8h

CU00925332

Dangerous deceit

The miners and tunnelmen contracted by the Water Board were used to danger and maiming and, occasionally, death. Accidental death, not murder. Gerry Daniels, a miner, a man well liked by his mates and an explosives expert, was the best of his kind and lived life to the full. When his body was found at the bottom of the shaft a suspicion of foul play brought DCI Ian Roper to the scene.

Roper's first serious lead came with the discovery of bloodstains in the boot of the victim's car and, more importantly, the absence of a jack from the otherwise immaculate set of tools. The victim's popularity was legendary but despite interviewing the many men with whom he worked, no more leads were forthcoming.

However, a different investigation got underway when an unreported crime came to light and members of two local families became suspects, each with a motive for wishing Daniels dead.

While *cherchez la femme* remained the prime concern for the Rickenham Green CID, a hidden drama of human weakness was hurrying to a fateful conclusion.

This is the fourth in Janie Bolitho's unputdownable DCI Roper series of whodunits.

DANGEROUS DECEIT

Janie Bolitho

Constable · London

First published in Great Britain 1995
by Constable & Company Ltd
3 The Lanchesters, 162 Fulham Palace Road
London W6 9ER
Copyright © 1995 by Janie Bolitho
The right of Janie Bolitho to be
identified as the author of this work
has been asserted by her in accordance
with the Copyright, Designs and Patents Act 1988
ISBN 0 09 474240 5
Set in Palatino 10 pt by
Pure Tech Corporation, Pondicherry, India
Printed and bound in Great Britain by
Hartnolls Limited, Bodmin, Cornwall

A CIP catalogue record for this book
is available from the British Library

For tunnelmen and miners everywhere

1

Ian Roper, Detective Chief Inspector at Rickenham Green for more years than he cared to count, had been around a bit. That is to say, he had heard and seen many things in his time. Some of them were irksome, many of them were obnoxious. But what he was encountering now was outside his experience.

The men with whom he needed to converse and those whom he was required to interview spoke a different language. His vocabulary increased overnight. He was picking up the jargon fast. He had to.

When he had first read of the proposals in the *Rickenham Herald*, it had not occurred to him that the operation would require his involvement. It had not occurred to the men themselves, either. They were used to danger and maimings and occasional death. Accidental death, not murder. Once the body at the bottom of the shaft had been examined, the possibility of it being the former was immediately ruled out.

'Will it affect us much?' Moira Roper had asked when she read the article and studied the enlarged section of the town map printed on the front page.

'What's that, love?'

'I thought you'd just read it. About this EC thing, clearing up the beaches. It says that most of the work'll be down on the coast but that larger underground pipes are needed to carry the sewage and any excess flood water. We don't get floods here. What're they talking about? They'll be digging up the roads again.'

'Digging up the roads, causing traffic chaos and God knows what. They've only just resurfaced Saxborough Road. It's always bloody chaos, the way this council's ruining this town . . .'

'Oh, don't start on about that again, Ian.'

His face was a trifle sulky as he got up to switch on the television. He couldn't help it, he had to drive through the town twice a day and often more. The new traffic system was one of the bugbears of his life.

'It says they're starting next week. Where do they get all the men from?'

'How should I know?'

'I'll be in the kitchen, ironing. If you want me.' Moira shut the living-room door with quiet deliberation.

'Damn it,' Ian said to himself. The argument had started last night and was obviously not over yet. He had not spotted Moira's conciliatory overtures. It was such a trivial thing. Moira was out with her friend, Deirdre, had warned him she'd be late and asked him to put the bin out ready for the morning. The dustmen collected from Belmont Terrace early. He was asleep when she came in, having forgotten all about it. She had undressed rather noisily and mentioned that it was not a lot to ask. They slept a foot apart. Their rows were infrequent and mostly caused by his forgetfulness. He knew he ought to apologise. After he watched the news.

Ian found verbally apologising to his wife extremely hard. He made her a cup of tea instead. She recognised the act of contrition and by bedtime reason was restored.

Whilst DCI Roper went about the routine of *his* job, men

from the main contractors reported to the Water Board their geological findings and suggested the best, and cheapest, type of equipment necessary for the mammoth task. With the traffic division of the police they planned the routes over which the heavy plant would be transported. They liaised with sub-contractors and engineers until, finally, everything seemed to be coming together, and they prayed that this would not turn out to be one of those ventures plagued with problems.

The main contractors, Nelson Enterprises, were going to use their own tunnelling team, backed up by miners.

All the local authorities were aware exactly when the cranes and JCBs and portable offices were being brought in. Notices were posted everywhere warning the public when the roads would be temporarily closed. At least in Rickenham it would not be for the duration of the work, as occasionally happened.

Jack Harrington, project manager, was satisfied. He sat back in his chair and lit a small cigar, one of the many he got through in a day. He and Peter Macey, his second-in-command, decided they had covered everything and celebrated with a mug of tea and a Danish pastry.

A week later the wheels were in motion. On a wet and dreary Sunday afternoon the portable offices were towed into place. They came from different depots and their various colours signified which part of the organisation they belonged to. The bright yellow of Nelson Enterprises had a board on top, shaped like two sides of a triangle and bearing their logo.

The cranes were unloaded; their drivers were due to arrive later that night or first thing in the morning.

All over the country men were packing and saying goodbye to their families. Some were already on the way.

Colin Jordan and Tom Clancey were two of them. They were known in the trade as travelling men. Over the years they had come to know hundreds of others like themselves. They greeted each other by place names and dates, often instead of names. Their verbal shorthand consisted of phrases such as 'Manchester, '79. You jacked if I recall,' or 'The Jubilee Line, wasn't it?' They rarely forgot each other, no matter how little time they spent together or whether they got on. They were special because they were different. The jobs were transitory, lasting two weeks or five years. Their existence was outside most people's recognised world.

As the older ones left, to run pubs or to retire or to die, the stories about them became apocryphal.

Tom Clancey was the first to arrive. He came by train. Nothing was new, nothing was strange. There were few counties in England and Wales he had not worked in.

There had been a delay. Tom had expected it, as it was a Sunday. 'First things first', he told himself. It was twenty minutes to ten, bleak and cold, and a shower of sleet welcomed him to Rickenham Green. He was not prone to preconception so was neither expecting nor surprised to walk out into the shabby-looking streets surrounding the station. What he noticed first were the lights and the creaking sign of the Station Arms. It was more than a pub. Inside there was a reception area, the red, patterned carpet threadbare and no one in sight. He pushed open one of the swing doors to his left. The top half was of frosted glass. The bar was massive. Seated at intervals along the wall were three or four customers. Two men stood at the bar in conversation with a plump woman nursing a half of lager.

'A pint of Guinness, please,' Tom said, dropping his holdall on the floor. In it was all he ever required. Some underwear, a couple of T-shirts, a pair of jeans and a clean shirt and his rigger boots. Overalls and protective clothing came with the job.

The woman poured the drink. Tom grimaced as it rushed from the tap and settled quickly. He knew, before he took the first sip, that the Guinness would be thin and tasteless. He would not be doing his drinking here. In a day or two he'd know the ropes: the cheapest shops for food, the best pubs. For tonight he must settle for whatever he could get.

'Do you know any places for bed and breakfast?' he asked.

The woman sized him up. He was sober and clean and didn't look like trouble. 'I can put you up here. How long for?'

'Tonight, and possibly tomorrow night.' By then he would have spoken to the others. Someone might be looking to share rented accommodation; someone would certainly know where to get good bed and breakfast.

'Ten pounds,' she said, 'including a decent breakfast.' The price was reasonable as he wasn't sharing. He'd been four to a room before now.

'That's fine,' he said.

'Where're you from?'

'Leeds.'

She laughed. 'Funny sort of accent for Yorkshire. Definitely the Emerald Isle. My husband was a Cork man. He's dead now. Good thing in a way. He didn't live to see what a dump this place's become. Still, no point in doing anything about it now – it's coming down soon, just like everything else. God knows what I'll do then, I'm too old to turn my hand to anything else. Another pint?'

Tom was surprised to see his glass was empty. There wasn't time to find another pub and he didn't want to offend her because he needed an early breakfast. He took a piece of paper out of his back pocket. 'How far away am I from . . .'

'Saxborough Road?' She smiled at his expression. 'I knew it the minute you walked in. I put up a crowd of lads before, when they were building the bypass. Did you come by car? Well, you won't have seen it yet. So you're

here for the "clean- up"? You'll be wanting an early breakfast then – is six thirty all right?'

'That's fine, lady.'

'The name's Gloria.'

'I'm Tom.' They shook hands.

The second Guinness didn't taste as bad. He ordered a
third.

'How do you get these jobs then?'

'Through the grapevine mostly. Word of mouth and
reputation.' They knew, before the *Construction News* and
other papers came out, just what was going on where. 'Do
a bad job and everyone knows. No one'll employ you.
Works the other way too.' Everyone had their own book
full of contact numbers, from project managers, to sub-
contractors to the men themselves.

'How long're you here for?'

'As long as the job takes. Six months, maybe more.'

'You can have another drink when this lot's gone,' she
said confidentially when she came around the bar to collect glasses.

Tom shook his head. It was a tempting idea but he was
tired. He had enough experience to know Gloria didn't
fancy him but even so, he was not in the mood for late-
night chatting.

She showed him the bathroom and gave him a room key.
'You won't be disturbed – apart from me, you're the only
one here.'

Tom wondered how she could live alone in this mauso-
leum. His bedroom was large and very cold. He slept, as
he always did, in his underwear and shirt.

All over Rickenham were notice-boards displaying plans
and explanations of exactly what was happening and why
and the benefits to be gained. Even so, by midday, the
Water Board had already dealt with numerous inquiries

and several complaints. The residents could hardly be blamed. It seemed to them that as soon as their ears had stopped ringing from the thuds and clatter of pneumatic drills and the rumble of cement mixers, they were to be subjected to more noise and inconvenience. No one remembered the petitions and committees they, themselves, had organised to clear the town centre of congestion – which the bypass they demanded had somewhat remedied. The old residential and warehousing area down by the station had been an eyesore for years. What an awful introduction, the residents claimed, for those people who arrived by rail. Most of it had been demolished now; office blocks loomed skywards and a row of rather chic shops stood where railway workers once lived.

'We're doing our best to cause as little inconvenience as possible,' Jeremy Saunders, spokesman for the Water Board, soothingly repeated over the course of the day, then listed the eventual benefits for those who, impossible as it seemed, had missed the enormous amount of publicity concerning the operation. 'Thank you for calling. I've made a note of your complaint.' This was true. He had to in the event of any court action following. Jeremy looked at the sheets of paper on his desk and tried to assess how high that pile would become before they had finished.

Colin Jordan arrived at the site at 7 a.m. on Monday along with the other men. Introductions were made, the hierarchy established. The agent went through the safety regulations, which they all knew and sometimes ignored. 'And if I catch anyone without a helmet, you're sacked.'

No one responded; they'd heard it a hundred times.

The offices were clearly designated, the canteen operational. This, too, was portable and large enough to hold four trestle tables, a sink, four electric burners and a hot-water urn. On their breaks the men would cook for themselves, mostly meat: fried steaks or chops and eggs. Within a week the place was filthy. Splattered grease covered most surfaces and the floor could never be clean, not with mud-encrusted boots and dried, white cement powder. Cigarette ends were ground indiscriminately into the mess.

Because the agent's name was Neil Thomas people assumed he was Welsh. He wasn't, and he didn't like the Welsh as a people. This was no real criticism of the Celts – he disliked almost everyone. He hated the job and, at times, hated life itself. Just because things were going well, it didn't mean they would continue to do so. He sighed as he imagined all the things which could go wrong; he was already counting the cost of the penalty clauses which would come into force if his fears were justified.

He sat at his desk studying the intricate plan of the tunnel, although he had almost memorised it. It was not the tunnel he was visualising, it was something quite different.

Daylight was still an hour away. The site, surrounded by high boards and wire mesh in the cause of public safety, was now called the compound. Halogen lights lit the scene, and the white or yellow hard hats of the men were gleaming. The reversible yellow and black protective jackets were almost identical to those of the traffic police and glimmered luminously in their newness. Watching the scene, seeing nothing, Neil Thomas thought of what might be. The peace of the bitter January day was shattered as machinery started up.

Routine became established, faces were already familiar. The shaft was down. Skipfuls of soil then harder materials were brought to the surface and removed in lorries. The same was happening down on the coast. Eventually the tunnels would meet up, the pumping stations would be set in motion and the sewage of Rickenham Green would be recycled or returned to the sea in a pure condition. The beaches would be safe and clean.

These environmental considerations did not enter the heads of the miners and tunnelmen. To them a tunnel was a tunnel, be it for sewerage, for carrying cars beneath mountains or rivers, or for transporting millions of passengers a year below the chaos of city streets.

Gerry Daniels was a miner and had been all his working life. If there wasn't another tunnel waiting somewhere to be built, he thought he might as well give up. In the good old days he'd mined for coal in Yorkshire and Wales and had spent one year in Australia. Mines were closing everywhere but there was still plenty of work underground. The change-over had not been difficult. He was well aware of the distinctions, of the cliques formed between miners and tunnelmen, but he didn't give a damn. To him there was only one difference. In a mine you followed the seam, in a tunnel you worked to specifications dictated by a laser beam. Rock was rock, whatever its propensity, and if it needed shifting, Gerry Daniels was more than happy to oblige. He was an expert with explosives.

Over the years he had broken almost every bone in his body. There had been rockfalls, cave-ins, runaway locos and chains which acted like an octopus. There had also been pub fights. He loved his work and he loved his life. His hardness was legend, as was his capacity for drink.

Two ex-wives did not know whether to be sorry or glad they were no longer married to him, and the five children he had produced along the way idolised him. He was likeable and liked and he found much to laugh at.

On the rare occasions he contemplated death, he imagined his would come beneath hundreds of tons of rock. It would be a fitting end.

At least part of his wish came true.

It was Gerry Daniels' body which was found at the bottom of the shaft during the coldest February for nineteen years.

2

The Dixon family lived in a modern house situated on the curve of a cul-de-sac in Frampton, a village eight or nine miles north-west of Rickenham Green. It had never been a village in a true sense, just several cottages lining a stretch of road. There was no square, no church, no pond.

Over the years the row of dwellings had multiplied in both directions then branched off, as if bored with continuing in a straight line. Some enterprising resident had applied for, and received, planning permission to turn his front room into a shop, the kind found in every English village and, quite often, at the end of back street terraces in towns and cities.

Now, as then, the shop sold every imaginable necessity but it had been enlarged, modernised and remodernised until it resembled a miniature supermarket. Other shops existed and, twenty-seven years previously – recently, compared with the age of the original cottages – a disused boathouse had been converted into a pub with living accommodation above.

The Dixons' house, along with the other eight detached houses in the cul-de-sac, was ten years old. They were its second owners. The overall impression was of squareness: the building itself, the windows and the patch of lawn in the front. Inside it was no different from millions of other homes. It had all the usual facilities, without extras, and all the blandness of modern architecture. To the Dixons it represented security, success and happiness. The rented accommodation in Rickenham where they'd brought up the girls was a dump.

'Lay the table, will you, Nicky? Dad'll be here soon.'

'Oh, Mum, I'm just watching . . .'

Marie Dixon walked from the kitchen to where her daughter was sitting in front of the television set in the lounge. She pushed a button and the screen was blank.

'Oh, all right then.'

'Don't sulk. Come on, you don't want Dad to come back to you like this.'

Marie and Phil were strict parents who believed in certain rules and regulations for their children. They understood that kids liked to know exactly where they stood. If they didn't, how could they break those rules and test themselves against their parents, seeing just how far they could go? The girls were loved and secretly worried over. So much could befall teenagers now.

Marie watched Nichola sulkily placing knives and forks each side of the cork table mats. These days her mouth seemed to have settled into a perpetual pout. She also seemed to be on the verge of anorexia, the way she toyed with her food.

'Here he is.' Marie heard Kate thundering down the stairs and they almost collided in the narrow hallway.

'Dad.' She threw her arms around him. An immature thirteen-year-old, she had no hesitation in displaying her emotions. Phil hugged Kate then kissed his wife, a slow, lingering kiss, followed by a wink. Nicky stood in the lounge doorway, a look of disdain on her face.

'Nicky? No kiss, eh?' Dutifully she brushed her cheek against his. It was sickening, this display of family unity, this breakfast cereal advert image they had of themselves. She hated the predictability of it and all the hypocritical, middle-class values her parents defended. She was certain she was the only one who was aware of the real situation.

'Where did you go, Dad?' This was Kate, of course, full of interest and curiosity.

'Holland.' Phil related a comical version of the delays experienced at Customs, omitting the parts where he lost his temper, a temper kept hidden from his family for whom he would do anything. All he wanted was their happiness and he believed he had just done something to achieve this, to prevent them drifting away from each other. He had sensed a certain tension in the air on his last couple of times home yet, superficially, everything seemed all right.

Nights like this were a bonus: returning to Larchfield Close, a meal waiting and the anticipation of going to bed with Marie. With daughters of thirteen and fifteen they mostly had to wait until bedtime.

This time, though, Nicky seemed a bit quiet.

'What's up, Nick?'

She smiled through gritted teeth, hating to be called Nick.

'Nothing.'

Phil glanced at Marie, who shook her head. Phil thought he got the message. Fifteen. Her period, no doubt. How wrong he was.

'Everyone finished? I've made a treacle pudding.' Marie put the three empty plates in the sink and scraped the remains of Nicky's food into the pedal bin. She made no comment, not tonight with Phil just home.

'Nicky?'

'Not for me, thanks. I'm full.' God, it was awful. Despite all their pretensions her parents were so unsophisticated. Treacle pudding of all things. Nevertheless, she remained seated until they had all finished. Bad manners were frowned upon. Punishment had never been handed out physically, but her pocket money could still be stopped. And she needed it. This week more than ever.

'It's amazing, isn't it?' Moira commented as she dished up their evening meal. 'I can't say I've ever noticed a Water Board van before, now you can't move for them.'

Ian was still rubbing his hands. The latter part of the afternoon had been spent outside following a long spate of burglaries from garden sheds and sheds on two sets of allotments. Garden tools and machinery were expensive, the thieves had known what they were doing, and they had picked the right time of year. February, with the ground frozen solid and no right-minded person outdoors if he could help it, let alone gardening, was perfect. Lawnmowers and hedge trimmers and machines for shredding leaves and wood and weeds were cleaned and oiled and lying unused and unobserved. One man had said he only checked his own shed when he read about it in the paper. He had no idea when his strimmer, secateurs and shears had gone missing.

By four thirty Ian felt he could have written a book – two books. One on garden tools, another on owners of garden sheds. Sensibly clad in thick socks, and an extra jumper, his sheepskin over the top, he was still frozen. The tips of his ears were numb and he suspected his hands would never be warm again.

'Stop shivering, Ian, you're making me feel cold.'

'It's not exactly warm in here.'

'The heating's on. Perhaps you're getting a cold.' Moira was flushed with the heat from the cooker. 'This'll sort you out. Sit down.'

Under his nose was a plate of steak and kidney pie, potatoes and vegetables. Steam rose in appetising curls. Ian loved her meals – except when she produced things she and Mark preferred, such as salad and pasta. Conversely, Moira loved seeing him clear his plate.

After a few mouthfuls, Ian slowed down. 'Mm, the pastry's delicious.'

'Thanks.' Moira smiled. All those years when she didn't work, when she spent whole afternoons baking and cooking, taking great pride in the fact that she didn't take short cuts or use anything out of a tin or a packet – and this was the first compliment for ages she had received verbally. An empty plate was always a compliment. The family-size steak and kidney pie had been purchased in Safeway's with fifty pence off because its expiry date was tomorrow. Of course, she had taken it out of its foil container and put it in the lid of a Pyrex casserole dish to disguise its origins.

'What were you saying just now?'

'Oh, just that there's blue and white vans everywhere. Still, it's not causing as much disruption as I thought. I imagined the whole town centre being dug up.'

'That's because, being a typical female, you can't read plans.'

Moira did not bother to retaliate. He could think what he liked – she knew where the real power lay under the roof of 14 Belmont Terrace.

'It's hard to believe they're blasting down there. I thought we'd feel the vibration.'

'It's controlled. And it's over a mile away. Fancy going out tonight? Barry said he's taking Lucy up to the Feathers about nine.'

Moira hesitated. There was the last of four hour-long episodes of a serial she was watching on the television and they did not possess a video recorder. 'Yes,' she said, 'it'll make a change.' Mostly she complained they didn't go out enough.

'What's Mark up to?'

'He's out somewhere with Tina.' Tina was his latest and, so far, longest-lasting girlfriend. It frightened Ian, the way his son was growing up.

'It seems warmer,' Moira said as they walked back from the pub.

'I don't think so. It's the effects of the drink. Look at the cars.' A thick layer of ice made patterns on windscreens and the pavement glistened with frost. The grass on the verge between the trees was white and spiked like a punk's hair-do. There was a stillness in the air as if the world was holding its breath, as if under this hard, frozen exterior living things were taking stock, preparing themselves for the thaw and spring when they could burst through the soil.

Indoors, Moira put the kettle on and Ian reset the central heating timer. If it was like this in the morning he wanted to make sure more than the chill had been taken off before he got out of bed.

Shift workers waited at bus stops, stamping their feet, their arms folded and tucked beneath their armpits, their faces pinched and blue with cold. Litter lay motionless, newspaper and take-away wrappers stiff with frost like pieces of abstract origami. Tom Clancey, who had decided to stay on at the Station Arms, walked past the bus stops, oblivious to the cold. His skin was toughened from outdoor work. Six forty-five. There was little traffic about. Headlights were reflected in the blackness of shop windows; the overnight lights of the compound were directly ahead. The crane loomed high over the boards and fencing, its chain wound back to a few feet, the hook barely moving at the end of it.

He went in through the open gate. Colin Jordan, the crane driver, was already seated, a thermos beside him. He saluted Tom with a wave, his voice inaudible over the noise of the engine, his own ear-plugs preventing him from hearing any reply. By now they were a team – they had to be, they were totally reliant on one another. Tom put his carrier bag in the canteen. It contained a large, white, sliced loaf, butter, tea-bags, milk and a bacon joint Gloria had boiled for him yesterday afternoon after the bar was closed. He was comfortable there and knew now that accommodation didn't come any cheaper. And the breakfast was something else. Gloria knew how to feed a

21

man. He did, however, do most of his drinking elsewhere. Gloira put this down to his wanting to be with his mates.

Tom rammed his helmet on to his head, slipped his arms into his waterproof jacket, and made his way to the yawning chasm which was the top of the shaft. The ground was still hard underfoot; later, as the ice melted, the compound would turn into a quagmire. The circular safety wall around the shaft was approximately four and a half feet high and was an extension of the metal rings which lined it to the bottom. In clear view of the crane driver was a small, wooden platform upon which Tom stood to make his signals in either direction.

The underground workers were straggling out of the canteen and in through the gate. Tom hooked the cage they called the man-rider to the crane and checked the connection. Four men got into it and shut the gate. It was a four-sided affair, the sides coming up to an average man's chest. Four metal bars extended upwards from the corners; overhead was the connection which attached it to the crane. Tom went over to his platform and stood on it, about to give Colin the signal to wind the men up, move them over to a spot above the shaft and lower them down. First he looked down to make sure nothing had inadvertently been left at the base.

The shaft was lit down the whole length of its fifty-yard drop.

His hand was still raised, ready to give the signal, when his head whipped back again. There was something down there.

'Jesus, Mary and Joseph!' he said. It was a man. If not dead, then unconscious.

'What the fuck's going on?' Alastair Menzies shouted from the man-rider. Other obscenities followed. They meant nothing, it was the way they communicated.

Tom walked over to them. 'Someone'll have to go down alone. There's a man down there. Certainly injured, possibly dead.' He saw by their faces that they didn't believe him. Then they realised who they were dealing with. Tom Clancey was a serious man, a steady man; he did not go around making jokes like this.

'It'd better be me,' Terry Grant said. He was the first-aider amongst the group. 'And you, Alastair.' As lead miner, Alastair was responsible for the men. 'Get Colin to drop us down but to stop a couple of feet from the base.'

The other two men got out of the man-rider.

Colin's brow had furrowed in puzzlement. Unable to hear, he had no idea what was going on. Whatever it was, he did not so much as put the clutch in until and unless he received a signal from Tom. Tom, his banksman, was his eyes and ears.

At last the signal came. The two men were lifted and swung slowly in the direction of the shaft. The man-rider paused above it, then was gently lowered. Colin knew, from experience, from the feel of things, that they had not touched the bottom. Later he would find out what was happening. For now men's lives depended upon his actions.

It was seven twenty when the emergency services oper-ator connected Neil Thomas's call to the police. Gerry Daniels had not died in company time. He did not know what difference that made, but he clung on to the fact. Even Neil, who was inclined to panic, recognised that Terry Grant and Alastair Menzies has done the right thing, had not, for once, acted as miners and instinctively brought the body up.

Detective Chief Inspector Roper almost knocked his glass of water off the bedside table when the telephone jerked him rudely awake. It was pitch dark. The luminous hands of the bedside clock told him it was seven thirty. Although the alarm was due to go off in fifteen minutes, it felt like the middle of the night.

Moira mumbled and turned over. She reached out an arm and found only empty space. Ian was sitting on the edge of the bed.

'What is it?' she asked, sitting up and reaching for her dressing-gown.

Ian ignored her. He listened for only a couple of seconds before replacing the receiver and pulling on his clothes.

'Do you want some coffee?' Moira called after him as he went to the bathroom to splash his face with cold water. He was regretting those two extra pints of Adnams last night.

'Half a mug, if it's quick.'

Moira ran downstairs, filled the kettle with just enough water to cover the element, spooned coffee into a mug and added two sweeteners. She ran back upstairs to switch off the alarm because she hated its raucous sound – but anything less and they were both inclined to sleep through it.

Ian's sheepskin jacket hung off one arm as he gulped down some coffee. He put the mug on the hall table where it duly left a ring, completed his dressing and picked up his car keys. 'See you later.'

There was no point in asking what that meant. Moira went upstairs to shower.

DCI Roper did not need directions to the compound. There was hardly a person in Rickenham who was not fully aware of it. To the east a band of light crept up over the horizon, the blue strip lighter now than the sky would be in full daylight. He parked the car and walked in through the open metal-link gates. A shortish man in a tweed overcoat and a hard hat approached.

'I'm Neil Thomas.'

Ian introduced himself and pulled out his identity.

'Nothing's been touched,' Neil said.

Ian wondered why he was already on the defensive. 'The man in question is in the tunnel, I believe?'

'Yes. Two of your people are down there already. Here.' He handed Ian a helmet. 'You'll have to wear this. Regulations. And be careful, there's still a lot of ice around.' Having a dead body in the shaft was more than Neil could cope with, an injured chief inspector as well would not do much for his credibility.

Ian peered over the side of the shaft. Oh, God, he thought. Do I have to? When he saw how he was expected to make the descent his stomach churned and he was thankful there had not been time for breakfast.

'I'll have to stay up here.' Neil beckoned to Tom Clancey who made the appropriate signals. As the man-rider left the ground Ian instinctively gripped the metal sides, cold as they were. His head swam. He had a paranoid fear of lifts. Yet once he was above that long drop he realised he was all right, that this was different. Then he saw why. It was because he wasn't enclosed. It wasn't lifts he need worry about, he decided, it was claustrophobia.

Four men waited at the bottom, besides the dead one. John Cotton, Scene-of-Crime officer, who lived a matter of yards away, and a PC Ian recognised but could not put a name to. By their outfits, the other two men worked here.

John Cotton did not appear in the least uncomfortable in his helmet. He pushed it back slightly and wiped his brow. It was unexpectedly warm down there. He raised his eyes and his shoulders in one hopeless shrug of despair. Quickly trying to adjust to his surroundings, Ian saw why.

The tunnel stretched in both directions, intermittently lit with bare bulbs running along one side of the curve at the top. Two rails ran along the bottom, hardly visible because of the four inches of water which had soaked, and probably ruined, Ian's brogues. Water was constantly trickling in from various points in the tunnel casing. Forensics were going to love this.

Gerry Daniels' body lay sprawled out; his clothes were soaked. There were two injuries to his head but there were probably other, multiple injuries if he had fallen down the shaft. From his position, it seemed a possibility. DCI Roper was not aware that, at that moment, only he and the PC thought it a possibility.

'You are?' Ian spoke to the nearer of the two men. When the rest of the team turned up, they would have to take it in turns near the body, retiring further down the tunnel or waiting on ground level.

'Terry Grant. This is Alastair Menzies.'

'And you discovered the body?'

'No, sir. The banksman did.'

'I'm sorry?'

'Tom Clancey. He gives instructions to the crane driver. He looked over the side before we started and saw there was somebody down here.'

'What did he do then?'

'He asked us to come and take a look.'

'Why didn't he come down himself?'

'He can't do that. He's a surface worker, and it would mean someone else acting as banksman. I volunteered because I'm the first-aider. We didn't know he was dead then. Alastair came too because he's lead miner.'

The terminology and relevance of all this would have to wait. There was a shout from above. They all looked up.

Dr James Edward Harris grinned at them from the top of the shaft. To a few he was known as Jim but most people, including his wife, called him Doc. When referring to him in the third person, it was The Doc, with capital letters.

'Unlike him to be so prompt,' John Cotton observed, 'especially at this time of day – the whisky hasn't usually worn off yet. Usually he's out delivering babies or whatever it is he's supposed to do, when we need him.' Needless to say, The Doc had one of his forty cigarettes a day in his hand.

Doc Harris was lowered down, seemingly oblivious to the strangeness of the situation. The five men already down rearranged themselves to make room for him. Ian, with his extra height, was stooping. He stood at six feet four inches. The tunnel was four inches too low even if he stood in the middle.

'He's dead all right.' Grant and Menzies exchanged a look. They thought that much was obvious, but they were not aware of police procedure.

'Do we need to stay?' Terry inquired. They might as well join the others in the canteen. Very little, if any, work would be done today. They'd stay, though. They were paid for the hours spent in the compound.

'No,' Ian told them. They got into the man-rider which hung waiting, and gave a shout. Tom Clancey looked down. Alastair, index finger pointing, waved his wrist in a circular motion, the signal to take them up. Tom repeated the sign to Colin who sat in the crane oblivious to what was going on.

'We'll need the Home Office pathologist.'

'You're sure, Doc?'

'Sure as I can be he didn't receive these head injuries falling down there.' The Doc nodded towards the top of the shaft where a murky sky was visible. 'See the skin here, where it's split? It's like a flap. Someone whacked him with something damn heavy. My guess is a metal object.'

'Has he been down here all night?'

'Difficult to say, especially in these conditions. He'd have been cold above ground, but it's warm down here – and all this water . . .' He sighed again.

'We may as well go up. We can only hope old Harry's a bit quicker than usual. There's no need for you to stay either, you can do your job just as easily at the top.' The Chief was addressing the PC, whose duty it was to record everyone's comings and goings. As there was only one way into the tunnel it was pointless him staying there. As for the various members of the team taking one carefully chosen route to do their business with the body, that, too, was a waste of time. The narrowness and the water prohibited such an action. And if Gerry Daniels had been thrown down, there would be no traces of the killer here, except any found on the victim's clothes.

'Photographers?'

'The duty inspector said he'd arranged it, sir.'

'Fine. Ah, how do we get ourselves out of here?' There was a ladder to the surface. No way was the Chief going to use that.

'Oi, you up there!' Doc Harris's deep voice echoed as he bellowed to the man above. Tom Clancey looked down. The Doc made a sign with his hand. It may not have been the correct one, he was pointing at the sky, but it was understood. A few seconds later the man-rider loomed over them and was lowered once more to a spot over the body, without actually touching it. The four men climbed into it.

'I'm sorry, constable, I can't place your name.'

'Joseph, sir.'

'Ah, yes.'

'Sir? It feels odd, somehow, leaving him down there on his own.'

'It does, doesn't it. Still, I don't suppose he'll mind. He's used to it.' The Chief studied PC Joseph's face. He looked sincere. He had thought for a second that he was saying it because he would prefer to remain in the warm even if he only had a corpse for company.

Neil Thomas saw them emerge and came out of his office. 'Can I get you some tea or coffee?'

'That would be very welcome. And one for the constable here, if that's all right.'

'Thank you, sir.' Joseph smiled his appreciation.

'Is there somewhere we can use to interview people?'

'My office, I suppose.' It was said with resignation. 'How long before someone comes to collect him? Daniels.'

'I've no idea. Depends how long the pathologist takes to get here and the SOCOs. Sorry, Scene-of-Crime bods.' The Chief couldn't resist it. They had their own jargon as well. 'Let me know when they arrive,' he added to PC Joseph, who was staring sadly at his shoes and the bottom of his uniform trousers.

'I didn't think, I could've organised you some boots,' Thomas told them belatedly.

'Never mind. All part of the job.' The Chief's smile was more of a grimace. His feet were like blocks of ice. At least the cabin that served as Thomas's office was warm.

'Gerry Daniels, what was he?' They had been given the name with the initial call.

'A miner. A good one.'

'Is there any reason for him to have been down there last night or early this morning?'

'No. None. We're not double-shifting yet. There's only the day shift which starts at seven.'

'And without the crane, the only way in is via the ladder. Oh, excuse me a moment, will you?' Through the dirt-encrusted windows he had seen two cars pull up beyond the fence. The men who stepped out of the first one he did not recognise, but they had to be the photographers because of the equipment they were carrying. John Cotton, who had remained near the gate, approached the other men who were part of his Scene-of-Crime team. Ian went to join them, wondering why John, usually so garrulous, had hardly said a word today. He was explaining the situation and its difficulties as Ian approached.

'We'll make a start. If we wait for Harry Ford we could be here all day. At least we can get the preliminaries done.'

John's team mates took in the scene above ground. This was bad enough. If it was as John described underground, they had little hope of finding anything.

'Are you okay, John?'

'Not exactly.' His face was pale and there were grey smudges under his eyes.

'Something troubling you?'

'These are hardly ideal circumstances. Oh, you mean apart from this. Actually, I've got a raging hangover.'

Ian laughed. He knew what that felt like. But John Cotton was not renowned as a drinker.

'It was our silver wedding anniversary yesterday. I'm not sure whether I was celebrating or drowning my sorrows.' His relationship with his wife was tempestuous. Ian wasn't sure how many times one or the other had walked out.

'I'll leave you to get on with it. I'm over there if you need me.'

He returned to Thomas's office. 'That round thing, over there . . .' He indicated the item in question by pointing. 'Does that cover the top of the shaft?'

'Yes.'

'So Tom Clancey – the banksman? Have I got that right? Good. He would only have seen Mr Daniels' body when it was removed.'

'No. It's only covered at weekends. The gates are locked at night and we've got a security man with a dog. No one can get in.'

But someone had. Two people. And one of them may not have been alive at the time.

'I don't understand what he was doing down there. He must've started to climb down, or maybe back up the ladder, and fallen. That's his car over there, by the way.' Outside the gates stood a grey Honda. 'There's no other explanation, is there?'

'I'm afraid there is, Mr Thomas.' But the Chief did not tell him what it was.

Doc Harris had driven off after a brief conversation with John Cotton, possibly advice on curing a hangover. The

Chief envied him, he would have time for a hot shower and a change of clothes before his morning surgery. Or would he? It was nine thirty already. And where the hell was Swan?

Detective Sergeant Barry Swan and he worked well together. Barry was his junior by some twenty years and, initially, he had disliked him for his flash clothes, his reputation for womanising and his arrogance and vanity. Now he understood him better. And speak of the devil, Ian thought, as he saw Swan's car pull right into the compound and come to a stop alongside a small caravan.

He watched as he picked his way across the ground, which was now beginning to thaw. Ian grinned. His shoes would be filthy. He banged on the window and beckoned him in, introducing him to Thomas.

'I'm up to date, sir.'

'Good.' It saved asking Thomas to leave whilst he filled Barry in.

'Now, Mr Thomas, you were saying?'

'Daniels was supposed to work this morning. I thought it was unusual for him to be late. He's always punctual – unless . . .' Thomas stopped.

'Unless what?'

He had put himself in a spot. No man was supposed to go down if they had been drinking or there was the smell of drink on him. Daniels was an exception. They couldn't do without him. There had been many mornings when he smelled of drink.

'Unless he'd been out on the town the night before.' And there had been times when he'd been drinking all night and come straight in to work. It was known that he kept a couple of tins of strong lager in the canteen which kept him going until he could sober up properly.

The Chief wondered if it had all been a mistake, if Daniels had been drunk and simply fallen. The postmortem would say for certain.

31

'Who would want to kill him?'

'Kill him?'

'That's what I said.'

'No one. That's ridiculous. He was well liked.'

'You mean amongst all the people who work here, no one fell out with him? Ever? No one had a grudge against him?'

'No. I know it sounds incredible, but as far I know, that's how it was.'

'Was he married?'

'Yes. No. Divorced, I think.'

'We'll need to see his personnel file. The next-of-kin has to be informed.' And would have to identify the body, even though any man in the compound could have done so.

'The files are at the coastal site.'

'Okay. May I use your telephone?'

The Chief did so, arranging for someone to go over and get the details. He also requested several more officers to come and help with the interviews.

'Thank you. We'll need to speak to each man in turn. May we use your office? And we'll need another one if that's possible.'

Thomas said he would arrange it.

'I also need the name and address of your security man.' It would certainly be interesting hearing what he had to say. Thomas told him the name of the firm and the man's name, but didn't know his address.

Harry Ford, the Home Office pathologist, did not arrive for another two hours. When he had finished with the body, he confirmed what Doc Harris thought. Harry, a more cagey man, only said he believed it was likely Daniels could have been killed before he was put in the tunnel.

The SOCOs completed their unsatisfactory work and packed up.

Neil Thomas heaved a sigh of relief when the body was finally removed. Gerry Daniels' exit in the man-rider was not the most dignified. It was nothing, though, to what the pathologist would do to him.

3

Neil Thomas was unusual in that he lived locally and only had a few miles to travel to work. Marg, his wife, hated him staying away. Apart from a couple of times during the course of their married life, he had returned home each evening, even if it involved a round trip of as much as a hundred and sixty miles.

When they moved from Colchester it had been in their minds to buy somewhere close to the sea. When they started looking at properties nine years ago it was winter, the weather almost as bad as now. After three days of being stung by hailstones and fighting against an easterly wind sweeping off the sea, with sand in every crevice of her grossly overweight body, a ruined perm and a streaming cold, Marg decided somewhere inland would be more suitable.

Their bungalow was a couple of miles from Frampton, in an even smaller village. Widdersham had an advantage over its neighbour: it boasted two pubs.

Thomas was nothing if not consistent. He was in awe of Jack Harrington, the project manager, as he was of anyone in authority; he was frightened by the men under him because of their hardness and their reaction to any criticism; but he was terrified of Marg. And now, more than ever, he had reason to be.

When he collected her from her shopping expeditions to Rickenham Green he watched with a sinking feeling in the pit of his stomach as she waddled massively towards the car, full carrier bags clutched in hands which reminded him of the jaws of a JCB. Thomas wondered if he hated her. Marg did not hate him, far from it. He dreaded bedtime, when she would cream the make-up from her face, climb into a voluminous, but transparent nightdress, then slide under the covers, the mattress sinking in protest. He would lie rigid, waiting for her hand to move to his thigh, then higher. He would close his eyes and ask himself how on earth it was possible he had become aroused.

Marg was not in the least self-conscious. She would stand in front of the full-length mirror, smiling coquettishly at her reflection, pushing her perm this way and that, believing she was as attractive to her husband as the first day they met.

Until recently, Neil Thomas's life had been dull and boring and predictable. Work was an escape from Marg, but it brought its own headaches. Then, one night, about five weeks ago, he, too, had stood in front of the mirror and scrutinised himself. At forty-eight his body was in good shape. It was lean and hard, although dressed he looked a little stocky. His hair was strong and thick, the colour of unpolished steel. Until then it hadn't struck him that he was quite a handsome man. Marie Dixon obviously thought so.

It was his habit to call into the Black Bull for one or two pints – never more – before returning home. On that evening one of the miners had given him such a mouthful of abuse he couldn't face the regulars, knowing exactly what each would say and when they would say it. For a change he went into the Dog and Duck.

He ordered a pint of beer and a rum chaser. He was aware that he'd handled the situation badly and probably deserved the man's antagonism, but he had really believed he was in danger of being thumped. He had only just stopped shaking.

34

The woman behind the counter was pleasant and polite and would not have looked out of place behind the counter of Marks & Spencer. She was well groomed, her make-up discreet, her blouse V-necked, but not revealing, and her skirt came to below her knees. He put her in her mid-thirties. There was a wedding ring on her left hand.

'I haven't seen you in here before,' Marie said, chatting because there was only one other customer and he was reading a newspaper. 'Just passing through?'

'No, I live here. I usually go to the Bull.'

'So do lots of others. I hear the beer's cheaper.'

'Not by enough to matter.'

He discovered that she worked a couple of nights a week and most lunchtimes and that she had two daughters who stayed with their grandmother on the evenings she was there.

After that he took to having his drink there on the two evenings she was on duty. When she touched his hand he knew it was not accidental. It started from there.

Thomas could not wait until the double-shifting started – he'd have the perfect excuse to be late. The only problem was they had nowhere to go. Too risky at Marie's, with the neighbours and the risk of her children coming home, and he could hardly ask Marg to disappear for an evening. They used the car, driving out somewhere and leaving the engine running and the heater on. It was sordid, but he didn't care. It was so very different from balancing himself on Marg's bulk. For the first time he experienced snatches of happiness and felt himself lose ten years.

This evening was not one Marie worked. He wanted so much to talk to her but it would have to wait until the morning when he could ring her from the office.

The ground froze another few inches deeper as night descended, and the forecast promised no signs of change in the foreseeable future. By five thirty the sky was black with an orange glow from the lights of the bypass in the distance. There was a limit to how much information could be taken in even if it was being recorded. Ian realised he was becoming stale and thought it best to give up for one day. 'I'm afraid we'll be back in the morning,' he told Thomas. 'We haven't seen everyone yet.'

Thomas was not happy, but it could have been worse. Gerry Daniels' body had been removed at two thirty; he had only lost half a day's work.

Even in this weather a lot of pedestrians stopped when they came to the compound. They peered through the mesh fence and watched the men going about their mysterious business. They stared at the crane as it dropped men down or brought them up, fascinated, as people always are, by large pieces of machinery resembling prehistoric monsters. They did not stop because they knew what had happened. Some would hear it on the news, others would only find out late that week when the *Rickenham Herald* came out. No doubt a lot more would stop then.

Barry Swan and Ian Roper went back to headquarters in their own cars. DC Campbell and DS Markham returned in the pool car in which they'd arrived together.

'A bit out of the ordinary, this one,' Alan Campbell remarked when they'd been debriefed. 'A sod of a job for forensics, I should think, but at least we've got facilities.'

This was definitely an advantage. They had taken over Thomas's office as the incident room; it was similar to one they sometimes needed to tow into place. A radio caravan was installed in the compound and they were able to use the tiny kitchen in Thomas's cabin or the main canteen, providing their own supplies.

'So what do we know?' the Chief asked Barry as they made their way to the Crown, the oldest pub in the town, which stood on the edge of the actual Green. Their breath, along with their cigarette smoke, streamed ahead of them.

Barry pulled out a handkerchief and wiped his nose. He laughed at Ian for wearing a hat, saying it was old fashioned. His own blond hair was nowhere near as thick as his superior's. It was longer at the back – much – but the top was definitely thinning. It irked him more than he ever let on, this hirsute disparity. That, and Ian's height. Beside him, in his long, loose, expensive raincoat, Barry felt like a dwarf.

'No good making guesses yet,' Barry said in answer to his question. 'We've still got more people to interview. No shortage of them this time.'

'Mm. Did you read the security man's statement?'

'I could've written it myself. Just what we expected. God knows why people bother.'

Ian had sent a detective sergeant round to interview Harold Phillips, the security man, because his part was crucial. He had, presumably, been in the compound when whatever happened happened. At the same time Ian was not holding his breath. He had a pretty good idea in advance what Phillips would say. He was not proved wrong.

DS Emmanuel and a PC had driven to Phillips' house as soon as they had elicited the address from the security firm for whom he worked. They drew up outside a mean-looking terraced house, one of many which were almost identical. Built in the days when rail transport ruled, they were well constructed of brick but the dull paintwork was peeling and there were dustbins in the tiny patches at the front which could not be described as gardens. There were no trees lining this street and the impression was of re-spectable poverty.

32 Normandy Road, a little after nine fifteen, and the female occupier opened the door in her dressing-gown. 'Oh,' she said, 'I thought you were the postman. Oh,' she said again, looking startled and gripping the revers of her robe, pulling it tighter round her neck, the skin of which

had lost its elasticity. Even so, for a woman obviously in her late fifties, she was attractive.

DS Winston Emmanuel, big and black, smiled his most winning smile, the one that had turned many a girl's legs to jelly when he worked in Birmingham. He knew, here in Rickenham, that people were a little wary – he was definitely in the minority. There were Indian and Chinese restaurants, their owners and families and staff no longer an unusual sight in the streets or the shops, but tall, black Africans were few and far between. When Amarilla got off her ass and divorced her layabout husband, he hoped she would join him here.

Rose Phillips was surprised on two accounts. She had no idea what this smartly dressed black man could want with her, then she saw the uniform of the second man. She was confused and a little scared until Winston smiled. It wasn't bad news, then. She smiled back.

'Mrs Phillips?'

'Yes.'

'Is your husband in?'

'He is but he's asleep.'

Winston introduced himself and the PC. 'I'll have to ask you to wake him, madam. It's very important we speak to him.'

The sooner the questions were asked the less time Phillips would have for forgetting or making up excuses. There was, of course, the possibility that Phillips was the murderer. He had had the opportunity and the means – there were plenty of metal objects lying around on the site.

'Stuff gone missing, is it?'

'Does stuff normally go missing when your husband's at work?'

'Of course not, I just assumed it must be something like that.' But colour had crept into her face. 'I'll go and get him.'

They were shown into the living-room, where she put on

one bar of an electric fire by kicking the switch with a slippered foot.

The carpet was wearing thin in the middle of the room and the furniture was old and heavy. On the mantelpiece were a couple of ornaments and some curling postcards. Despite the general air of dilapidation, the room was spotlessly clean.

It was six or seven minutes before Phillips appeared. They had heard the toilet flush and running water. No doubt he'd needed to splash his face to wake himself after only an hour's sleep.

Harold Phillips' dressing-gown was brown and made of wool and tied with a plaited, cotton cord, a style Winston did not think was made any more. His sparse grey hair had been combed. 'Make us a cup of tea, will you, Rose?'

Rose went obediently out of the room, making no complaint and showing no desire to listen to what these strangers wanted of her husband.

'I'm sorry to disturb your sleep, sir, but we need to ask you some questions relating to last night.'

'Of course. Excuse me, do have a seat.'

'Thank you. Can you run through exactly what happened, from the time you went in?'

'Yes, but what's happened? Is something missing?'

'No. Perhaps if you answer the questions first it might be easier.'

'Certainly. Anything to oblige the boys in blue. Citizen's duty and all that. I can tell you exactly, nothing wrong with the old memory. I got there about six thirty. I start at seven, officially; by that time all the men are up. When they've gone I do my rounds. You've seen the place, I expect – it doesn't take long.'

'And this is what you did last night?'

'Indeed. Then I retire to my dug-out, as I call it. Quite comfortable, considering. It's warm and I've got a kettle and my colour TV.'

'I see. What then?'

'I make another check, about midnight. It's well lit, I don't need a torch or anything. It's not a bad little number. As I said, I've got the TV, there's some good films on late at night, and I read a lot.'

'Did you see or hear anything out of the ordinary?'

'No. Nothing. Only the usual things.' He stopped.

'Such as?'

'The men going home. That's all I meant.' DS Emmanuel did not believe him. He guessed that if Phillips had heard or seen anything, he'd have stayed put in his cabin. 'If anything's been taken, I certainly don't know about it. I may not be as young as I was, but my reactions are probably just as good as when I was in the army. I could tell you some –'

'I'm sure you could, sir. Then how is it, do you think, one of the men was found at the base of the shaft this morning? Dead.'

'What?' Phillips' hand shook as he stood up to reach for his pipe which was lying on the mantelpiece. 'It's impossible.'

'It's true, I'm afraid.'

'He must've been there all night then, since before I got in.'

'No. We know he left with the other men and he was seen some time later.'

Harold Phillips sank into the cushions of his chair, a defeated man. He was bound to be sacked. He would never get another job now. It had taken long enough to procure this one. Life had hardly been worth living since his retirement from the army. All the time he thought back to his tours abroad, when Rose went with him, the perfect army wife, entertaining, and both of them enjoying every minute. They had not thought ahead to the time when it would end, when Harold would have to live on his services pension until he was entitled to a state one as well.

40

They had no friends in England, only each other. He knew how much Rose missed the other army wives. They had nothing in common with their neighbours here and it would be the same wherever they lived. 'Ah, Rose, my dear. Thank you.'

Rose placed a tray on the teak-veneered coffee table. It was beautifully laid with a white, lace-edged cloth and all the crockery matched. The cubed sugar was in a bowl on top of which were a small pair of tongs. The milk was in a jug. She poured for them all.

'Someone's been found – oh, is it all right if I tell my wife?'

Winston nodded. It would be on the local news, possibly at lunchtime. Phillips did not know the identity of the man.

'Dead?' Rose repeated when she knew why her visitors were there. 'But surely you'd have seen something, dear?'

Phillips shook his head. 'I didn't. I didn't see a thing. Will I lose my job?' He looked at DS Emmanuel. There was an expression of such pleading misery in his eyes, Winston guessed how much it meant to him. It was the one bit of pride left, that he could still go out and earn a living.

'I don't know. That's up to your employers. As far as we're concerned it doesn't seem you've done anything wrong.' The PC glanced at the DS, surprised to hear him make such an admission. Possibly the old boy had had the television on too loud to notice anything, or, more than likely, he'd dropped off to sleep.

'One more thing, Mr Phillips. Surely the dog would've growled?'

'Sheba? She's at the vet's for couple of days. She's old now, Sergeant, and to be honest, she's more company than use. I think her hearing's gone. Mind you, the sight of a German Shepherd is enough to frighten some people.'

'All right, Mr Phillips, we'll let you get some sleep now. If anything does come to mind, give me a ring.' Winston

41

handed him a card and thanked Rose for the tea, then they left.

Ian and Barry took their drinks to a table near one of the fires. Another reason for liking the pub, apart from its excellent pint of Adnams, was the presence of a real fire at both ends. The smell of wood smoke filled the air. Even when the door opened to let in another customer and an icy blast followed, it did not last long. There was, however, a draught seeping under the half-curtains at the windows behind him. Ian asked Barry to change places without explaining why.

They stayed for a second drink, then Barry said Lucy was expecting him home for something to eat.

Ian shook his head. The vanity was still there, the clothes the latest fashion, but a lot of the old Barry Swan was disappearing. He was gradually losing a drinking partner. He might just as well go home himself.

He was doubly disappointed to discover no one at home. Mark, all right, at seventeen, and due to start college in September, he didn't expect to see much of, but lately Moira was out a lot.

'I blame the job,' he muttered to himself. She had changed, imperceptibly at first, more noticeably lately. Once, it had crossed his mind she might be seeing another man. Her initial indignation, followed by scorn, when he challenged her cut him down to size.

He poured another drink and sat down with his brief-case at his feet. He would take another look at his notes, see if he could make anything of the facts so far.

Nichola Dixon was not expected home until ten past nine. To and from school she and her sister, Kate, made use of the council-funded bus which collected senior children from all the outlying districts of Rickenham Green. Many of these villages retained their own infants and junior school. In time, no doubt, that would change; for the moment, until they reached the age of eleven, children did not have to go into the town to receive their education.

On evenings when there were extra-curricular courses and clubs schoolchildren had to rely on their parents to collect them or use the ordinary bus. The service to Frampton was good as far as these things went: there was one bus an hour until eight forty-five with the last one at ten twenty. Nichola was expected on the eight forty-five, and would be on it. Not once had she caused her parents worry in that direction. On the rare occasions she missed it, she telephoned immediately and waited for her mother to tell her, in an exasperated tone of voice, that she would pick her up.

Tonight there was Drama Club at four o'clock. This lasted an hour. Nichola was chided several times. 'What's the matter with you this evening? You knew all your lines last week, but now you're so wooden, it's as if you're reading the lines for the first time.'

'Sorry,' Nichola muttered. Her interest in drama at the moment was concentrated on the real-life one she might have to face.

At five she almost ran from the school building and round to Debbie's house. Debbie's mother waited on tables in a hotel in the evenings, leaving her daughter to her own devices as her husband had disappeared five years ago. He was no great loss to either of them.

Debbie had left school at the first opportunity but was still unemployed. Nicky had ambitions to go on to university. Her teachers knew this was far from an impossibility. She worked hard, was well behaved and popular, just as she was at home, never causing any anxiety. What none of these people knew was that she had a secret life.

There was no doubt she had the body of a woman, but it

was not often realised there were times when she also had a woman's head on her shoulders. There were things of which she was aware that were supposed to be secret.

Her concern now was her parents' reaction if they found out her own secret. Her mother, hopefully, would act predictably by shouting at first then calming down and trying to find the best solution. Her father was an unknown quantity. He went out of his way to make things nice for them – she appreciated that, even if it was not a way she agreed with. But could a man be so totally unselfish? Would the knowledge of what she had done bring him out in different colours?

Nicky used people, she knew that, and thought them fools for allowing her to do so. Debbie and Paul, for instance. But the tables had been turned and she was hurt, more than hurt. How could something which had been so good suddenly end? Had he guessed? Was that why he was avoiding her?

It was no use torturing herself. There was an alternative. She tucked her long, dark brown hair behind her ears. Her eyes, equally brown, were huge and limpid and they, together with her sensual mouth and creamy, clear complexion, turned men on.

'Debbie'll know what to do,' she reassured herself as she headed in the direction of her house.

4

It was now known that Gerry Daniels had been married and divorced twice. Both ex-wives were extremely shocked and very upset to learn of his death. His children, three from the first marriage, two from the second, were inconsolable. He had kept in touch with them all although both wives had remarried. None of these relatives appeared to have any reason to wish him dead.

The senior Daniels were also out of the question: Gerry's father had died some time ago and his mother was in an institution, suffering from senile dementia and completely unable to understand what the pretty WPC was talking about. In the confusion caused by this unexpected visitor, she wet herself for the second time that morning. In the end it was Jason, Gerry's oldest son, who said he would make the identification.

His family details had been on file but there was no record of an up-to-date address. For the job he was staying at the Plough, a roughish sort of pub about three-quarters of a mile away. He had not turned up for the job until the Monday morning so the Red Lion, less than fifty yards away, was already full, the more organised men having arrived by opening time on Sunday evening, found the compound and gone for the nearest place to it.

DCI Roper discovered that the three men he shared with worked on the coastal part of the operation, which meant a trip down there to see them.

'So far we know that Daniels left work on Monday, earlier than usual, along with Alastair Menzies, Terry Grant and Jim Ryan,' DCI Roper recapitulated. 'What's a caulker, by the way?'

DS Swan, who was driving, shrugged. 'I thought they worked on ships, keeping the water out or something.'

'Ah. Same thing then.'

'Pardon?'

'Keeping the water out. All those rings – they have to be sealed, I suppose.' The tunnel was constructed of huge cylindrical metal tubes.

'Well, they're not doing a very good job of it.' Barry had been down to see where the victim's body lay. Rather spitefully, Ian had not warned him it was a trifle damp underfoot down there.

'We know these four men left together and went to the Red Lion. We don't know if he returned to his accommodation, and that I find very strange indeed, considering he shared with three men.'

'Well, that's what we're going to the seaside for, isn't it? To ask them.'

'No need for sarcasm, Swan, and please take these bends a little slower.'

'I'm only doing thirty-five. Much slower and we might as well walk.'

'I shall not buy you lunch in the Plough if you don't show a bit of respect.'

'I can hardly wait. I wonder if anyone's wiped down the tables since last I was in there.'

Ian grinned. It definitely wasn't his sergeant's type of pub.

'It's incredible the way no one's got anything but good to say of this man. I don't think I've ever come across a case like it. There's usually someone wants to put the boot in, some rival of whoever's dead who can't wait to blacken their name.'

'Perhaps we'll find out in a minute.' Barry pulled up by the open gates of the compound. This one was much larger than its counterpart in the town and the security was better. They were stopped and produced their identity, even though they were expected, before they were shown to the project manager's office.

A wintry sun had appeared in the sky earlier, but had once more retreated behind a bank of fast-moving cloud. Although a wind came off the sea, the temperature was a few degrees higher than it had been the previous couple of days. This ensured that the puddles were no longer sealed with ice. They crunched as the two men walked over them. The mud was mixed with sand.

There was a lot more machinery visible here and many more cabins. Jack Harrington's was part of what

46

amounted to a complex. They mounted three wooden steps. A girl, working at a word processor, saw them through a glass partition and came out to show them where to go. The accommodation might be temporary and portable but there was a small conference room, several offices, a kitchen and, near the entrance, an open area forming an L in which were displayed diagrams, maps and photographs showing how the scheme worked and the progress being made. There was even a small-scale model of the operation.

Jack Harrington stood up and shook hands. He was strong and athletic-looking with a wide smile and a hank of brown hair which flopped engagingly over his forehead. This place, as in Rickenham, was more than adequately heated.

Harrington came round the desk. He wore a pink and white striped shirt, the cuffs folded back to his elbows, and grey slacks with a belt; he was beautifully shaved. He looked every inch a city businessman until Ian's eyes rested on the trouser bottoms. They were creased and mud-splattered where they'd been crammed into boots.

'Have a seat, gentlemen. I'll organise some coffee.'

He returned a minute or two later. 'Now, the last permanent address we have for Mr Daniels is that of his second wife. Correspondence goes there. It's a scam. They all do it and think we don't know.'

Ian frowned.

'It's not worth explaining, it doesn't have anything to do with his death. It's how they go about claiming extra travelling expenses, if their permanent address is over sixty miles away.' Harrington fumbled in his drawer, a look of near-panic on his face. 'Ah,' he said, 'I thought I'd run out.' He lit a cigar. Ian, who had made many unsuccessful attempts to give up, was pleased to see a fellow smoker. He took his cigarettes out of the pocket of his sheepskin. Barry, who claimed it would take at least a full-frontal lobotomy to make him stop, did likewise. Harrington slid the ashtray to the centre of the table just as the coffee arrived.

'It's quite likely that Mr Daniels didn't have another address of his own. From what I know, he usually cons some female into taking him in until another job turns up. He's good. Was good. A rogue, but I liked him.'

Barry and Ian made brief eye contact. Was it going to be the same here? Everyone liking him?

'I take it, by your continued interest, that he was murdered?'

'It's a suspicious death. We have to treat it as such until we know otherwise.' Which Barry knew meant that they were not one hundred per cent certain and that they'd find out this afternoon after the post-mortem.

'I didn't get much sense from Neil Thomas. He's inclined to panic,' Harrington said.

'We believe Mr Daniels shared accommodation with three of the men who work here.' Ian looked at his notes. 'Tony and Paddy Malone and someone called Seamus. Apparently he's known as The Goat.'

'Ah, Seamus McGinty.' Harrington did not clarify further; he merely smiled. They would find out soon enough. McGinty was aware of his nickname but assumed it had connections with a song made popular by Val Doonigan about a man who shared his second name and was in possession of such a creature. The truth was somewhat different, as anyone who was downwind of him realised immediately. Rumour had it that he must have been badly frightened by water at some point in his life.

'Do you want to see these men now?'

'Please.'

Harrington picked up the internal phone and stabbed out three digits. He spoke briefly, then replaced the receiver. 'McGinty's on his way. I'm afraid the Malone brothers are in the tunnel and there's a load of concrete going in. It's physically impossible for them to come up at the moment.'

Harrington knew that letting the Chief Inspector use his room for the interview would cause less disruption but he decided against it. He picked up the phone again. 'Peter, are you tied up at the moment? Good. There are two gentlemen from the police here and they need somewhere to conduct an interview. Fine. You can come in here with me.'

'You bastard,' Peter Macey said to Harrington some time later as he ineffectively wielded air freshener and opened the window despite the weather. 'You knew, didn't you?'

'Markham can go and see them later,' Ian said when they were back in the car once more, having gulped in lungfuls of fresh air once they were out of the company of Seamus McGinty. They had waited for an hour, then given up. Harrington was telling the truth when he said the Malone brothers could not come to the surface. They still had to speak to the landlord of the Plough and there was the post-mortem to attend.

Barry pulled into the car-park. There were only two other cars. They must belong to the landlord and his wife, Ian thought, because they were the only customers.

'Yes?' the man behind the bar said. Brian Greenham was aware of the situation and knew the police would be back. He hardly knew Gerry Daniels, he saw so little of him, but he was glad he hadn't been killed on his premises. What was worrying him was how much his lodgers had said about his highly unorthodox licensing hours. 'What would you like?'

Barry said he'd have a lager and inspected the glass before he took the first sip. Ian ordered a pint of bitter, thinking it was the invisible germs which got you in the end.

'Not a bad drop,' he said, holding the glass up to the light. 'Sell much of it?'

'Not these days – mostly lager.'

'And a fair bit of Guinness at the moment, I'd imagine.'

Brian Greenham was right. These two were old bill.

'It's certainly good for trade. As you can see, there isn't much of that at the moment. If things don't pick up this year, I'm retiring.'

The time had come for official introductions. These out of the way, Ian said, 'Did Mr Daniels return here on Moday night?'

'I've already been asked that. I don't know.'

'How come?'

'Monday's my night off. Me and the wife go out, always have done. My daughter looks after the place for us. The lads've got a key to the side door. We got back about twelve thirty. I didn't hear anything after that.'

'We'd better have a word with your daughter. Is she here?'

She was and came downstairs. 'Two of them were in the bar until closing,' she said, 'the two brothers. They're always together. The other one,' she wrinkled her nose in distaste, 'he went up early. I didn't hear anything after I went to bed. Mind, my room's at the opposite end.'

It seemed improbable that no one was lying. Under that roof, certainly from twelve thirty onwards, had been Brian Greenham and his wife, their daughter, McGinty and the two Malones, and two other men who also worked down on the coast.

By the time Ian and Barry left – having refused the offer of a sandwich because there was the post-mortem to face – they began to see how it could have happened.

Seamus McGinty had told them he was tired and went to bed early. 'It's a man's job down that tunnel,' he said. 'A few pints and something to eat and I sleep like a log. Have to be up before six, too.'

It was confirmed that he was in bed early, but not

50

because he was tired. He was so drunk, according to the landlord's daughter, that the Malone brothers had had to carry him up and place him under the covers, fully dressed, at ten fifteen. He would have been oblivious if the murder had been committed in the same room.

The daughter would not have been watching out for Daniels – why should she? She had the pub to run single-handed and, if she had thought about it at all, she might have assumed Daniels had been elsewhere and let himself in through the side door. Ian had questioned the safety of this arrangement but the door only opened on to a flight of stairs. There was no access to any of the bar areas or the kitchen.

The landlord and his wife had been drinking elsewhere and stayed for one or two extra with friends who ran another pub before returning home by taxi. They, too, no doubt, would have wanted nothing more than to reach their bed.

This only left the brothers. It would be interesting to hear what they had to say.

'I think it's just like they're saying,' Barry commented once they were back on the road. 'If what McGinty told us is right – that he serves them drinks until they fall over or fall asleep – it's hardly surprising none of them knows what the others are up to. And, don't forget, McGinty said that Daniels wasn't with them all the time, that he did his drinking elsewhere too.'

'Pity he couldn't tell us just where.'

'Oh come on, Ian, I thought that would cheer you up. You could have a pint in every pub within a five-mile radius and find out.'

'I hope this post-mortem's particularly nasty,' was the Chief's only response.

Debbie had not been as helpful as Nichola had hoped. She had gone to the house and, as usual, they had drunk quite a bit of vodka. They stuck to that because Debbie said you couldn't smell it. At six, after they'd finished work, Wayne and Paul had come round. There were only two bedrooms but even Debbie was not brazen enough to use her mother's. She always took Wayne to her own room; Nicky and Paul stayed downstairs. She had told Paul she was sixteen, which she would be in another couple of weeks. He'd believed her – had, in fact, thought her more like seventeen.

Once or twice they'd smoked pot. Nicky didn't think much of it, she didn't seem to feel any different, but it affected Paul, or he acted like it did. He had been quite adventurous, for him, when he made love to her. He might be older than her but she was sure he wasn't as experienced.

'He's dead keen on you,' Debbie told her. 'He never stops talking about you. He even says things like wanting to meet your parents. You could do a lot worse.'

Nicky knew she could do a lot better. She already had. But none of it was relevant. This was just something to pass the time, her own secret rebellion, until she went to university. She could never explain this to Debbie, who thought such a plan a total waste of time. Debbie wasn't even trying to look for work, and her mother gave her money to supplement what she got in the way of benefits because it was easier and caused fewer rows.

Nicky, despite her protests against her parents' way of life, their trying to better themselves, was a snob. She would not be seen out with Debbie, nor with Paul come to that. He was fairly good-looking, and she had to admit that, even against her will, he did make her laugh. His brand of humour was sharp and acid and was learned on the streets.

Debbie's argument was true in a way. A man with looks and humour and a job he took seriously, and who had never been in trouble, was hard to come by. But Paul lacked something, something Nicky believed she had found, except it had all gone wrong.

Nicky had not mentioned her plans to Paul. She was afraid he might laugh if she spoke of a university place, which showed how little she knew him. He would have been proud. He would also have told her he'd wait for her. But Nicky didn't want any such ties. The world was hers. She would rule it if she could. First she had to solve the problem which was causing her to lose sleep.

5

The post-mortem, as these things go, was not too bad. Ian turned his head away, as he always did, on two occasions. First, when the large Y-shaped incision was made from each shoulder and down the abdomen; then again, when the flesh was peeled back from the skull. He was used, now, to seeing human organs being moved around like pieces of meat.

The pathologist had successfully fought for, and been given a microphone; this was placed directly above the body, not only enabling him to give senior police officers the facts verbally, as he came to them, but also saving someone having to make notes. The whole thing could be typed straight from the tape.

Some of the tests were immediate; others had to be sent off to the lab, in which case it might be days or weeks before the results were known.

'The head injury', the pathologist told them, leaving out most of the technical terminology he used when speaking into his microphone, 'was inflicted some time before the other injuries. I would say your assumption is correct. He was killed before he was dumped in that tunnel.

Instrument? Heavy, definitely metal. There are small particles of rust, et cetera. Can't say what, forensics can do their bit. A lot of scar tissue, none of it new. Steel pin in his left tibia, should have been removed years ago. Quite hard, these miners, I believe – probably couldn't be bothered once he found he could walk all right. All the other contusions and abrasions were after the time of death. And on that, I'm afraid, as usual, I can't be of much help.'

'We know he was alive at 7 p.m. on Monday and dead at 7 a.m. on Tuesday.'

'Then you're lucky. Considering the outside temperature, the temperature inside the tunnel and the fact that the body was moved after death, I couldn't have even pinned it down to a twelve-hour range. Well, that's it, folks. Fancy a shot of something?' The pathologist walked towards the cubicle which passed as his office. The answer would be yes – with Roper it always was.

'The Doc would've loved this one,' Ian said as they sipped a malt whisky. 'Pity he couldn't be here.'

'Are you refering to the PM or the booze?'

'Both, come to think of it. I meant the PM. You confirmed what he said and what Harry Ford hinted at.'

'Ah, Harry. A cautious man if ever I met one. And a grandfather again, I believe. His children seem to breed like rabbits. Well, on to the next one. Motor-bike accident.'

They were glad it was over. Neither Barry nor Ian could understand why men deliberately chose to follow such careers. 'It's a science,' the pathologist once said, 'not a career.'

'What now?'

'We find out just where he ate that meal.' The stomach contents showed that food had been ingested less than three hours before death. What that food was they had yet to find out. 'We'll try the Red Lion again. Seems the most likely.'

They were aware that the men cooked for themselves in the canteen. If they did so it was usually in the morning or around four on the afternoon break. As Gerry Daniels was still alive at seven thirty he must have eaten since.

Marie Dixon decided she would have a word with her elder daughter, but not until Phil was away again. She tried very hard to preserve a pleasant atmosphere in the house when he was there. She loved him, of that she was certain, and she didn't want to lose him. What was happening now, this affair with Neil, was something she could not bring herself to think about. She had drifted into it at a time when she was perfectly happy, when the sex with Phil was at its best. She could not understand it.

It's my age, she thought, the need for reassurance, that I'm still physically attractive. She knew a couple of her friends had had brief flings, then settled down with their husbands again. It was as if she was watching herself. It was another woman who got into Neil Thomas's car and let him make love to her. She had to end it and made up her mind to do so the following week. Except, she realised, I shall miss him in a way. He was so gentle, took so much time with her, and he was so damn grateful.

Marie heard the bus rumble to a stop at the end of the cul-de-sac. Less than a minute later Nicky came through the front door.

'Good evening? How's Sally?'

'She's fine. She sends her love.'

Marie kissed her daughter's forehead. 'Do you want something to eat? I'm just going to make Dad a sandwich.'

'No thanks, Mum. I've had something.' Marie doubted it but left it at that. Nichola might not be smiling but she looked better. There was some colour in her cheeks and a sparkle in her eyes. The evening at her friend's house had done her good.

DS Markham, clad in hard-wearing jeans, shirt and leather jacket, the uniform he wore summer and winter, made his way to the pool car-park. The only concession to the bitter weather was a white T-shirt under the other clothes. No one ever commented on his peculiar body thermostat – he never seemed to be too hot or too cold – because no one was ever surprised at anything Markham did. He was a loner, by choice, and if he did sometimes bend the rules, he was still recognised as a good copper. He was handsome, in a craggy sort of way, his hair uncompromisingly short, his eyes the blue of periwinkles.

At the Rickenham headquarters, the Chief had ascertained that Markham was in possession of all the facts before he sent him to interview the Malone brothers.

'They're our only hope, these two,' Ian said. 'If they can't tell us when Daniels was last seen, God knows where that leaves us. Do all these titles and machinery names mean anything to you? I'm struggling, I must admit.'

'Yes. My father was in construction.'

Ian almost dropped his cigarette. In eight years this was the first time Markham had volunteered any personal information.

'Tunnelling?'

'No. Roads mostly.' Markham dropped his eyes to his notebook. Clearly that was to be the extent of his revelations.

So Markham knew a bit about it. It might be useful – he could talk to the men on their own terms. Ian was becoming aware that, observant as he was, he was so accustomed to seeing gangs of men, helmets on, chests bare in summer, that it never crossed his mind to wonder what they were actually doing. Cones on the motorways, extra sets of traffic lights, these were just part of the inconveniences of life. He had no thoughts other than the typically cynical ones about workmen resting on their shovels. He had learned a lot in the past twenty-four hours.

Markham, true to form, had not set off for the coast until late in the afternoon. He had put in a few more hours on a case involving forged banknotes which were circulating the area, then, in his own time, requested a car and collected the keys.

The Chief had said the men were unable to come out of the tunnel. It could happen again. He waited until it was almost time for them to knock off.

He drove down the narrow roads in darkness, his headlights picking out the bare branches of overhanging trees. They were like ghostly arms, long-fingered and eerie. In the distance was the glow of the compound lights. As he neared them he recognised the throb of machinery as the pumps continued in their never-ending battle to keep the hundreds of tons of water out of the tunnel. His imagination told him what would happen if those pumps failed.

He parked, got out of the car and stood outside the drying room. His hands were in his pockets but he did not even shiver as arctic blasts swept across the compound, rattling chains and sending litter flying.

There were men on the surface. Markham knew his were still underground. After ten minutes or so the first lot came up in the man-rider. He watched as they approached him. 'Malone?'

'No. They'll be up in a minute.'

'Cheers.'

'Malone?' he repeated when the next four appeared.

'Yes, soir, that's us. Me and Tony here.'

'Okay. Have you got transport?'

Patrick Malone, known as Paddy, scratched his head. They knew the police wanted to interview them, but they didn't expect to be taken to the station. 'We have a lift with The Goat.'

Seamus McGinty's fame had spread. Markham knew who they meant.

'Get your stuff. I'll run you back to the Plough.'

'The Plough?'

'More comfortable there, don't you think?'

'I do, soir, I do indeed.'

The two brothers reappeared in a few minutes. Neither had commented on Markham's suggestion. They sensed that some of his ways were their ways. They knew a hard man when they saw one.

Paddy got into the front seat and chatted inconsequentially about the weather until they reached the pub.

The Malone brothers were both on the short side and squat. There, the resemblance ended. Paddy was the talker and, Markham suspected, the dominant one. He was dark and swarthy and, until he opened his mouth, could be taken for an Italian. Tony's complexion was paler and he bore the freckles which often accompany ginger hair and eyes of a faded blue.

'Guinness, is it?' Markham asked unnecessarily as the barman was already pouring it.

'It is. And the same for Tony.'

Tony smiled. He still had not spoken a word. Markham wondered if he was deaf and dumb. When he did finally speak, he realised why he said as little as possible.

They took their drinks to a corner table.

'You shared a room with Gerry Daniels?'

'We did. Us two and The Goat, isn't that right, Tony?'

Tony nodded and sipped his drink.

'Tell me about the last few days – say, from Sunday until Tuesday morning.'

'Sunday we don't work. We had a bit of a walk in the morning, down to get the papers and some smokes. Then we came back here and had a few drinks, didn't we, Tony?'

'S-s-s-sunday. W-w-we did, Paddy.' The last word came out in a rush, as if he was grateful he got it out at all.

Markham looked at him with sympathy. Nowadays a stutter that bad would be treated in childhood. He could guess at the Malones' background. He'd known others like it. They were from a large and poverty-stricken family, probably relying upon their own crops for food, and maybe the killing of one or two pigs a year. The older children took care of the younger ones. Markham bet these two were inseparable, had probably come over from Ireland together, and Paddy continued in the role of watching out for Tony.

'We stayed in here all evening, I believe.'

'W-we did.'

'And Daniels?'

'Yes. He was here. Sometimes he took a drink in other places. He was here Sunday.' Paddy Malone did not add that, after the lunchtime session, the landlord had locked the doors and the six of them staying there, plus a couple of locals, had continued quenching their thirst until seven when the pub officially opened again. Brian Greenham knew when he was on to a good thing and intended making money while he could.

'Monday?'

'We had our breakfast and went to work. Me and Tony and The Goat go off our way. Gerry's got his own car, he takes it into Rickenham. We didn't see him after that. I heard he went to the Red Lion with some of the others.'

What they heard was not important. 'Did he come back here on Monday night?'

'Never saw him if he did, soir. The Goat, well, he'd taken a drop too much. Me and Tony took him up – about half-past ten, I think it was?'

'Yes.' Tony nodded.

'We went up about twelve.' It was said without guile. Paddy was sure Markham knew of the extra drinking they did. 'I was asleep in no time. What about you, Tony?'

'M-m-me too. Asleep quickly.'

'And in the morning? Was he in bed?'

'No, nor did he take his breakfast. But you know, soir, a man like Gerry, no wife, well, he doesn't always want to be sleeping in his own bed now.'

'He had a woman?'

'That I couldn't tell you. If he did, he wasn't going to bring her back to the room.'

'Did he mention anyone, a name, maybe?'

'No. I saw him wave to someone once. It was the after-noon break, now, if I remember right. About four. It was dark, I couldn't see too clearly because of the compound lights in me eyes. It was a female –'

'Hang on. How could you? You work in different places.'

'Ah, didn't I say now? We were in Rickenham for the first two weeks. They got that shaft down ahead of us.'

'Any more men? During those two weeks?'

'No. Only me and Tony.'

'Sh-she was a s-s-s–' Tony shook his head. Whatever he wanted to say was lost. His vocal cords would not oblige.

'Smasher?' Markham suggested.

Tony smiled and his eyes lit up. He nodded and raised a thumb. Markham did not see Paddy lay a restraining hand on his brother's other arm and give it a warning squeeze.

'Another drink for you?'

Markham drained his glass and held it out. Why not? He'd paid for the first one.

'Will you take a drop of Guinness instead of that girl's drink?'

Markham said he would. When in Rome . . .

There was nothing more to be learned. If Daniels did have a woman they would need to find her. Yet in the statements he'd read so far, no one else had mentioned it.

After the post-mortem Ian and Barry made their way to the Red Lion. It was open all day which, in view of the fact that they were once more the only two customers, seemed a waste of time.

'My shout,' Barry said. 'A pint of bitter and – do you do coffee?' There was a coffee machine behind the bar with a few inches of murky liquid in the glass jug. Barry asked in case it was solely for the landlord's refreshment.

'Yes. Milk and sugar?'

Barry paid for the drinks, pulled off the top of the St Ivel dairy creamer without splashing his clothes and tore off the end of the sachet of sugar. Ian watched this performance and waited until he'd taken a sip. He grinned. He saw by Barry's grimace he'd been right – the coffee was lukewarm.

'Did you want any food? Only the girl's gone now. I can do you a sandwich.'

'No thanks. We're here to ask you a few questions, Mr Sprague.'

'Police?'

'Yes.' Ian produced his identity and told him their names.

'Again?'

'Sorry, but it's important. How well did you know Mr Daniels?'

'I didn't know him, not really. He came in with some of the boys after work but he wasn't staying here. Usually he left about eight. I imagine he went drinking wherever he was putting his head down. That's what most of them do.'

'I see. And on Monday?'

'Like I told your other man, he came in at seven, had a pint and disappeared.'

'Did he eat anything?'

'Eat? You must be joking. As far as I can make out those men work and drink. They don't have time for solids.'

'You're sure?'

'Yes. What's the big deal? Was he poisoned? If so, it wasn't by my food.'

'Did he ever come in with anyone else, someone he didn't work with?'

'No. Never.'

'You seem pretty certain.'

'I am. Same crowd every night. Like I say, what he did when he left here I don't know.'

'That was a waste of time,' Barry said as they made their way, once more, back to the station.

'Not really. If he didn't eat there, that takes us up to seven thirty – he must have had something later, which means he was still alive. Let's find out what Markham's discovered, then we'll leave it at that.'

DC Alan Campbell had spent the afternoon entering all that was known about Gerry Daniels and the men he worked with into the computer. It was programmed to cross-reference and cross-check all the information it received and to suggest the next course of action. So far they were still fact-finding.

They pushed through the revolving glass door at the entrance of the station, the runners swishing on the coconut matting. Warmth hit them and made their blood tingle. Already the stars were glittering coldly, promising another night when the temperature dropped well below freezing. Ian rubbed his palms together. Barry knew this was not just in order to get warm, it was a habit the Chief had of preparing himself before he really got stuck in.

'Coffee, I think, then a careful going-over of the facts. Where's my favourite WPC?' he asked William Baker, who seemed to be permanent duty sergeant as far as he could make out.

'Judy Robbins? Haven't you heard, sir?' Ian held his breath. Judy had babysat Mark when he was small; she was almost like a daughter to him. 'Her father died last night.'

'Oh no.' Ian looked at Barry. They were both aware how close that relationship was. He wondered if she would come through it. 'Do me a favour, Bill. When it's appropriate, find out when the funeral is and let me know.'

'Yes, sir, I'll do that.'

Barry was very quiet as they made their way upstairs. He and Judy had a longlasting feud. Because she was efficient, cheerful and assertive, fending off his chauvinistic remarks with ones of her own relating to his vanity and sexual prowess, they were often at each other's throats. Conversely, when they were working together, there had been occasions when they were perfectly attuned. Only now, on hearing this news, did Barry realise how much he liked her. He knew exactly what this would do to her and there was nothing he could do to help. His own parents were abroad and he hardly ever saw them. It was his grandmother who had brought him up and finally, when she died, left him the flat. Gerald Swan was a diplomat, his mother a diplomat's wife. He hardly knew them. He remembered the pain when his gran died, though.

'She hasn't got anyone else, has she?'

'No.'

They were both quiet while they waited for the coffee to be brought up. Suddenly Ian's enthusiasm had waned.

Ian made an interim report to Superintendent Thorne.

'I wasn't expecting much at this stage, Ian,' Thorne reassured him in his deep-voiced Birmingham accent. Mike Thorne was a younger man than might be expected to hold such rank, but he was liked and respected and was still near enough to having been on the streets himself to understand fully the problems and anxieties of the men under him. 'You seem to have an awful lot of people involved here. Any ideas?'

'None really. We're starting with the men closest to him– we've ruled the family out. There're other possibilities, a grudge from a previous job, maybe, somebody local he's upset. And we've not had any results back from forensics yet.'

Gerry Daniels' car had been towed away. On the Tuesday morning no more than a cursory glance had been taken through the windows. The door handles and boot lock could not be touched. All that could be seen was expected. Maps in a side compartment, mud on the floor and rough-looking clothing and some paperwork on the back seat. No obvious bloodstains or murder weapons.

'It's puzzling, though, Mike.' It had taken Ian some time to come to terms with the fact that the man in front of him preferred being called by his Christian name. Only in the privacy of his own office though. 'His car was there, but according to some of the men, not in the same place as where he parked it on Monday morning.'

'You think he drove back there on Monday night? Or someone else drove him back there?'

'It looks that way. And he was wearing his working clothes. Including his boots.'

'Which suggests, as you already know, that he didn't go back to his accommodation that night.'

'Yes, but if he was meeting someone, or going out, surely he'd have had a shower. Some of them aren't too fussy, I believe, but Daniels wasn't like that. Sorry, just airing a few thoughts.'

'Any time.'

'There's something else.'

'Yes?'

'WPC Robbins. Judy. Her father died last night.'

'Yes, I heard, Ian. I've arranged for flowers to be sent. She's on compassionate leave.'

'Do you know how he died?'

Ian got the answer he hoped for. 'Old age, if there is such a thing. Fell asleep in his chair early yesterday evening and didn't wake up. It was Judy who found him.'

Somehow that made it a little better. He had not suffered a painful, lingering death, and these days there were so many instances of old people being attacked in their own homes. He had met Fred Robbins and knew he would have put himself in danger, would have put up a fight. If there was a best way to go, Fred had gone that way.

'You look tired, Ian. Go home.'

Ian went back to his office. If he thought he was going to hear what Markham had to say, he was to be disappointed. Markham, on his third pint of Guinness, was indeed doing as the Romans do and Paddy Malone was regaling him with stories about tunnelmen.

DS Alan Campbell, satisfied that the computer knew as much as he did himself, decided to make a few more inquiries. He knew that Phillips, the night-watchman, was a slacker. It might be risking the Chief's anger, but he wanted to speak to him himself. He made his way across town to Normandy Road, guessing that at four thirty in the afternoon Phillips would be up and getting ready for work.

'Please come in.' It was Phillips himself who answered the door. 'I've been thinking about it. Perhaps I should've said before. You lot caught me on the hop yesterday. Sometimes there are other people on the site.'

'Oh?' Alan Campbell took out his notebook.

'Yes. You see, there's a caravan there. One of the men lives in it.' This was news. 'And sometimes – well, not often, but one of them has come back and gone to sleep in the drying room.'

'How do they get in, Mr Phillips?'

'The gate isn't always locked. And that's not down to me. It seems some of them have got their own key. It hardly matters. There's a big gap in the fencing at the back. They use that if they can't get in. Will I be in trouble over this? I was going to come and tell you anyway. My wife will confirm that.'

'Thank you for this information, sir.' DS Campbell ignored his question. Odd, no one else had mentioned the keys or the gap in the fence. Was it a mass conspiracy? He closed his notebook and looked up. Harold Phillips no longer bore any resemblance to the proud army soldier he'd once been. He was a scared and feeble old man. Campbell briefly rested a hand on his shoulder. 'I'll see myself out.'

He returned to the station and made a note which he left on the Chief's desk ready for the morning.

Tom Clancey was pleased he'd made the decision to remain at the Station Arms. He and Gloria got on like a house on fire. She was more than pleased to have someone else in the building at night.

'You look worried, Tom,' she said when he returned on Wednesday night.

'Not worried. Just thinking.'

'Something at work?'

'Yes. Gerry, the man that was killed.'

'Are they certain he was killed? Couldn't he have fallen?'

'Gerry? Never.'

'What's bothering you? Here, listen to me, and you without your pint yet.' She proceeded to draw it. Tom, having adjusted the spiggot slightly, found it a little more palatable.

'It was something I overheard. I think I should've told the police.'

'What sort of thing?'

'An argument. No, it couldn't've been much. Besides, the bloke involved is a real old woman. He's always getting people's backs up.'

'It's probably best to keep out of it. They'll find out themselves if it's important.'

'I expect so.' But it was preying on Tom's mind. He'd have a word with Colin. He smiled. Colin wouldn't have overheard. Up there on that big crane of his, with his earplugs in, only his eyes told him what was going on. Tomorrow then, he'd ask his advice. He was a big, sound, solid man, full of common sense, and he kept to himself. He didn't let the backbiting get to him like some of the others.

'Another pint, Gloria, and one for yourself. I'll make a decent landlady out of you yet.'

6

'You look exhausted.' Moira glanced up from her book when Ian arrived home, then took a second look at her husband. 'That bad?'

'Not really, we're ploughing through. It's not that. Judy Robbins' father died last night.'

'Oh, no, Ian. Oh, poor Judy. Is anyone with her?'

'I don't know. I've only just heard.'

Neither knew what to do. They had her telephone number but for Ian this was so unlike work. There it was his duty to intrude upon the relatives of the dead; when it was personal it was difficult to judge what to do.

Judy's mother had died when she was a small child. Her father had brought her up and eventually almost thrown her out because they were becoming too dependent upon each other. Judy's own flat was not far from his and they still went out for a drink together or played darts for the club. Or had done. She was an only child.

'Did Fred have any relatives, brothers or sisters?'

'I don't know. I've never heard him talk about any. Come on, Moira, get your coat. We'll have to go. If she's got friends or whatever there, all well and good. We can't just do nothing.'

'Mark! Come down a minute.'

He did so, running a hand through his blond hair, so much like his mother's.

'We're going out.' Moira wondered how her son would take it. Judy had looked after him so many times. 'Judy's dad has died. We're popping over to make sure she's all right.'

'I'll come with you,' Mark said, surprising both his parents.

WPC Judy Robbins, slightly overweight, short, dark hair awry, was in her early thirties. Between boyfriends – as she often was, possibly too conscious of all that could go wrong to settle with anyone permanently, too involved with the job to make many friends – Judy was in her nightclothes and alone. It was Mark who broke the ice by putting his arms around her. Tears sprang to Moira's eyes. Mark towered over her now, yet it seemed only five minutes ago that he was sitting on Judy's knee listening to a bedtime story.

'On your own?' Ian asked gruffly.

Judy nodded. She was extremely pale and her eyes were red-rimmed.

'Then get dressed, you're coming back with us.'

'No, I couldn't, I –'

'I'm pulling rank, WPC Robbins.' Ian smiled gently.

'All right,' she conceded. 'I wasn't looking forward to facing the night alone.'

Later, after Moira had cobbled together a meal and they were sipping brandy, Judy started talking, pouring out all her experiences with her father and her feelings for him. 'I'm sorry, Moira, I didn't mean to inflict this upon you. I actually think I could sleep now. Do you mind if I go up?'

'Of course not. You know where everything is.'

68

Judy smiled. 'There's one thing which surprised me – that bastard Swan turned up on my doorstep earlier. Lucy's good influence, that is. It's the first time I've ever seen him lost for words.'

'She'll be all right,' Moira said when Judy had gone up. 'She's tough. And she's probably right about Barry. He's a lot more human since he's been with Lucy.'

Ian looked at his wife. Slim and pretty and fifteen years his junior, she was an endless source of pleasure, even if he mostly forgot to tell her so. He was immensely proud of her. He was even secretly proud of the way she'd taken herself off on a course and got a job. With her education she could have done a lot better, but she'd chosen marriage to him over a career.

'Another brandy? It seems to be doing you good – you look a bit more perky now.'

'Love one.'

'How is it going, the case?'

'It's hard to say. There're so many people involved. What I'm really waiting for is forensics to finish with the blasted car. I've learned a lot, you know. You might complain about my hours, but the life these men live is amazing. Away from home for long periods, living out of suitcases half the time, cooking for themselves.'

'Cooking for themselves? Whatever next?'

'All right, no need for sarcasm, I could do it if I had to. And they spend half their life underground. But they seem to love it. Most of it's hard and dangerous work, too.'

'I know.'

'You know?'

'You seem to forget I work for a construction firm.'

Ian had not forgotten, he just had not considered the implications.

'A lot of the men are regulars, but there are others, here for one job, then off to another.'

Ian knew what she did, the name of the company and where it was. He often dropped her off at work. Naturally her knowledge of how the business ran must be increasing. There was a time when he had felt, in some respects, that he knew more than his wife. This was no longer the case.

'Can you be bothered with the late film?'

'No. I'm ready for bed.'

Kenny Kavanagh had been waiting to be interviewed. He knew they would get round to paying him a second visit. He was surprised they hadn't asked the first time. Whenever it was possible on a job, he towed his caravan into the compound, or as near to it as he was able, and lived in it. Once they were double-shifting, the higher-ups got round it by saying it was as well to have the sub-contractor permanently on the site. What he was doing was not exactly illegal, but it was frowned upon.

However, he had had one or two run-ins with the police before. He was not going to go out of his way to offer explanations before they were required.

DS Swan sat in Neil Thomas's office and waited for Kavanagh. He sauntered in and sat down.

'It seems that caravan belongs to you,' Barry said.

'It does.'

'And you sleep in it?'

'I do.'

'You didn't mention this when we spoke to you the other day.'

'No reason why I should.'

'I think there is. It means you were here the night Gerry Daniels was killed.'

'Monday night?'

'Monday night.'

'I wasn't.'

'You weren't what?'

'I wasn't here. I stayed the night with a friend.'

'Does this friend have a name?'

'She does. And she won't thank me for giving it to you.'

'I see. I take it your friend is married. I'll still need to know.'

'You don't believe me.'

'It's not a case of believing or otherwise. We have to check.'

'And if I refuse to tell you?'

'It could make things very awkward. For you, that is.'

Kavanagh sighed. It would make things even more awkward if he did tell them. Barbara would not be offering a repeat performance if her husband found out. He gave Barry her name and address. 'Look, she works in the baker's, just round the corner. Can't you go and see her there?'

'That where you met her?'

'Yes. We get rolls and pasties there sometimes.'

'All right. I'll do that. For her husband's sake. Not yours.'

Barbara Rawlings guessed why she was being questioned. Kenny had warned her of the possibility. 'Yes,' she said, when she'd taken him through to the back out of the way of curious customers and the woman she worked with, 'we spent the night together.'

'At your house?'

'No. At a hotel. And you can tell Mr Kavanagh from me, it's not an experience I wish to repeat. Tight-fisted bugger. I paid the bill.'

Barry made a note of the hotel in case they decided to follow it up. He felt that Mrs Rawlings was telling the truth and that she had no reason to cover for him, especially if she felt his treatment of her had been less than generous. What she did not add was that Kavanagh had paid for all their drinks – and Barbara could sink them –

and a meal as a prelude to taking her to bed. The meal had cost more than he spent on food in two months.

More time was wasted as each man in the compound was requestioned as to his whereabouts on the Monday night. No one, it seemed, had used the place to sleep that night.

'Don't ring me here again,' Marie Dixon hissed. 'Phil's here. I've got to go.' She heard his footsteps on the landing. 'That was Val,' she said in answer to the question in his eyes. 'I'd better go, I'll be late for work.'

'I'll come with you.'

Marie searched his face. Why? He had never done so before. Had he overheard her conversation? Like her daughter, she knew him to be a good, decent man. What would something like this do to him?

Phil pulled on a thick sweater. 'Won't you be cold?' he asked.

Marie was in a skirt and blouse, a mac over the top. 'No, it's only a couple of minutes' drive and it's always too warm in there.'

Phil sat in a corner reading the *Rickenham Herald*, which had been pushed through their letter-box earlier that morning. On the front page was a piece about Gerry Daniels' murder. THE BODY IN THE TUNNEL, it was headed. The statement Superintendent Thorne had given was not exactly riveting, just the usual stock phrases and a request for anyone with information to come forward.

Phil read it with interest. He knew all about the work that was going on in the town. He wished he knew as much about what was going on in his wife's head at the moment. He sensed she kept glancing in his direction. It was he who should be nervous. He didn't want her to find out what he'd done. Not yet.

There were no other customers for half an hour. A little after twelve they started dribbling in as lunch-hours began. By one fifteen it was quite busy. Marie continued serving drinks and another woman appeared at intervals bearing plates of food.

Marie was right, it was plenty warm enough. The heating bills must be enormous. A man pushed open the door. Phil was busy holding down the pages of the *Herald* which flapped in the icy blast that came with him, so he missed the expression of panic which passed across his wife's face. Neil Thomas walked up to the bar.

'What're you doing here? For God's sake, Neil, Phil's over there.'

'I just wanted to see you. I didn't know –'

'Didn't think, more like. You're supposed to be at work.'

'It's my dinner break.'

'Drink this quickly and go. If you do this to me again, it's over.' It was over anyway but now was not the time or place to tell him. A scene here would mean the end of everything.

'When can I see you?'

Marie was acting for all she was worth. Smiling at customers, including Neil, she poured drinks and took food orders. Phil must not see anything was wrong.

She calculated fast to get rid of Neil. Phil was going on Monday morning. 'Monday. Not before. And don't ring me. I'll wait in the usual place. Seven o'clock. Now, please go.'

Neil's heartbeat slowed a little. He'd thought she was going to finish with him. Now he had something to look forward to again. First, though, he had to survive the weekend with Marg.

As he drove back to Rickenham the bleakness of the weather seemed irrelevant. Since that first meeting with Marie it was as if the sun had not ceased shining. He spent hours lying in bed imagining how it would be, just the two of them. So far he had managed to overlook the fact that he would have to do something about Marg, who would not give up or give in that easily.

Neil Thomas had lived almost fifty years without learning a single thing about his fellow men. He had no idea what made people tick nor did he consider any of the possible reasons for their behaviour. Worse, he did not see this failing in himself. Which was precisely why he rubbed the men up the wrong way, and why he should have taken a lot more notice of what Gerry Daniels said during that argument.

Neil was jealous. He tried not to be but when he watched Marie being pleasant to the other male customers his stomach churned. And when he'd heard her name on the lips of Gerry Daniels he'd seen red. The man was dead and he deserved to die.

The husband was no great shakes in the looks department. No wonder Marie was bored with him – he'd sat there, nose in the paper, the whole time Neil had been in the bar. If it were him, he'd have been on a bar-stool, in the corner out of the way, but near enough to see her.

He had better call in at the coastal site. He had some paperwork to pick up and it was, after all, where he'd said he was going.

'What d'you think, Col? Should I mention it to the police?'

'They'll think it odd if you come out with it now. Leave it, is my advice. Besides, you only heard half of it.'

'But he said he'd kill him if it happened again.'

'Come on, how often do you hear that in a day? I've heard it said over a slice of bread in the canteen.'

'I know.' Tom Clancey sighed. It was true. Only this morning Alastair Menzies had helped himself to one of Terry Grant's tea-bags. 'I'll fucking kill you if I catch you at it again,' he'd said. It didn't mean anything, they didn't even associate the word kill with the murder which had taken place.

They were in the canteen now, on the afternoon break. One man was frying some black pudding and a couple of eggs, another was turning a T-bone steak, fat dropping on to the floor as he did so.

'Another drop of tea, Tom?'

'Yes.'

Colin limped over to the urn where boiling water was constantly available. He made the tea, dark and strong, and brought the mugs to the table.

'Where did you get that leg?'

'The limp?' Colin laughed. 'Dangerous work, putting out the milk bottles. Fell down the front steps and broke my ankle. Twenty-seven years on the cranes and never fallen off one, and you know what climbing up into them's like in this weather. Never been injured at work either. Just goes to show, doesn't it?'

Ian had time for only a glance at the front page of the *Herald* before he went to work. Mark was seated at the kitchen table, abstractedly munching a piece of toast.

'What'll Judy do now, Dad?'

Ian looked up, surprised. It was a rare thing for his son to utter a word first thing.

'She'll have a few days off to sort herself out. After that, it's up to time to do its trick.'

'Will she be staying here?'

'I don't know. If she wants to.'

'Only my room's bigger. I can stay at Tina's.'

This was not something Ian contemplated very often. The idea that his son might be having a sexual relationship made him feel very old and also very embarrassed. He did not think he could discuss it with him.

'Can you drop me off, Ian?' Moira asked.

'Yep. If you're ready now.'

'I am. Judy's asleep. I just looked in on her. I've left her a note.'

'Get on to the lab, will you, Barry? Don't let them give you the usual old stuff, they must have done some tests by now.'

The lab, true to form, did give him the usual stuff. Backlogs, more important cases. More important? Barry didn't argue, but in the end, yes, they had done some preliminary tests.

'Any chance of you telling me the results, or is it a secret?'

'That has to be Sergeant Swan,' the young woman who had been handed the call retaliated. 'No one else has quite your personal charm.'

'Ah, it's the lovely Sharon, isn't it?'

'No. My name's Brenda. Have you got a pen? Right. List of the car's contents: RAC road atlas, battered. Motorway road map. Same condition. Eighty-three pence in change. Four empty cigarette packets, Benson & Hedges. Fish and chip wrapper containing a few bits of batter and a couple of chips.' Barry was more than interested now. If those fish and chips had been Daniels' final meal, they might be able to discover where and when he bought them and pin down the time of his death. 'And before you ask, they are not compatible with the stomach contents analysis and the remains are at least a week old. Ash everywhere. Ashtray overflowing. Torch. On the back seat some recently worn clothes, mostly waterproof. Without damaging your eardrums with technical details, suffice it to say they aren't much good to us. No fibres adhere. Boots – we're still analysing the mud scrapings. And paperwork, all relating to various jobs and all of it out of date. Seems he used the back seat as his filing cabinet.'

'Is that it?'

'Be patient, Sergeant Swan. I'm reading the list in the order of our findings.'

'I'm so sorry, Brenda.' He stressed the last word. 'Do carry on.'

'Your fingerprint men weren't able to come up with anything. It's not surprising – that car hasn't been cleaned since it was new. However, the boot. A full set of tools, do you want me to list them?'

'Any relevance?'

'I don't think so. Only the victim's fingerprints, no blood-stains and all well looked after. Hammer, chisels, screwdrivers, saw, that type of thing. Spare tyre, new. Wheelbrace, clean. Grey carpet, slightly muddy and covered in blood.'

'What?'

'You heard me, Sergeant.'

'Why the hell didn't you say so right away? Daniels' blood?

'More than likely.'

'What does that mean?'

'Daniels is O rhesus-negative, not the most common group, so is the blood in the car. But as you know, our tests are a little more sophisticated these days.'

'Don't tell me. They break down the group further but they take longer.'

'Exactly. One other thing.'

'Yes?'

'The car was filthy but all the tools were, as I said, in good condition. Cleaned and oiled where appropriate. He had a new spare tyre and the wheelbrace.'

'And?'

'And there was no sign of a jack. Just thought I'd mention it, in case the inconsistency didn't occur to you.'

'Very kind of you, Brenda. Is that it?'

'Isn't that enough? I'll be in touch when we've finished. Cheerio.'

'In the boot?' Ian asked, incredulous. 'Someone stuffed his body in the boot of his own car? In that case, whoever it was drove to the compound on Monday night.'

'And our ever-wakeful night-watchman didn't hear or see a thing.'

'Have we double-checked house-to-house?'

'Alan Campbell's doing it. Knowing him, probably done it. I can't see much coming of it – there're mainly shops opposite, the upstairs accommodation used as store-rooms. The houses further down, well, the residents wouldn't be able to see what was happening the other side of the fencing. I expect –'

'Barry, I've just realised something. We've been assuming it was someone he worked with, but surely they wouldn't risk dumping him there, knowing Phillips was on duty? Too much chance of being seen even if he didn't come out and confront them.'

'It could work the other way. Whoever it was would know Phillips and have a ready excuse available for being there.'

'Really? Can you think of a suitable excuse for having a dead man about your person, one that you intend dropping down the shaft?'

'Not offhand, no. But why would anyone do it at all? The man's dead, killed in some unknown place, why not leave him there? He might not be found for days. This way his body was bound to be discovered almost immediately. And a local might not even realise there was no one there at night. He, or she, might think there's a night shift or something.'

'She?'

'You're the one always saying never discount any possibility. We don't know that Daniels had a woman, but knowing the sort of man he was, he probably did.'

'I can see that a female might deliver a blow with a heavy instrument, one hard enough to do the job, but how did

78

she get him into the boot of the car, let alone lift him high enough over the side of the shaft?'

Barry shrugged. 'Is it time to start asking around the pubs?'

'Yes. Have we got a photograph?'

'Daniels' son provided one. Taken six years ago but good enough for someone to recognise him still.'

'Fine. Sort it out, will you?'

'What exactly is this?' Ian asked suspiciously as he eyed a bowl of what, to him, looked as if it might have been scraped up from the ground around the crane in the compound.

'Houmous. Oh, Ian, don't do that.' He had stuck his forefinger into the dish and scooped out some of the contents, leaving an indentation in the neat swirls Moira had made with a fork.

'Mm. Not bad.'

'Yes, well, you're supposed to eat it with pitta bread, not with your hands which you haven't even washed yet.'

'You know what they say about a bushel of dirt. Or is it a peck?'

'Just leave it or there won't be enough. Shirley and The Doc are coming over.' She'd thought Greek would make a change. Kebabs were on skewers waiting to go under the grill. Ian would probably turn up his nose but would eat them just the same. 'Make yourself useful and open the wine. Red. They'll be here soon.'

Ian enjoyed the evenings they spent in the company of The Doc and his wife. Naturally, the conversation always began with work but Shirley was adept at getting them off the subject. She knew that her husband was an excellent GP in the old-fashioned way. He listened, and mostly got to the heart of the matter – which frequently was not what had brought the patient to his surgery. He rarely prescribed drugs but gave a diagnosis, a thing which was becoming rarer, and thus reassured his patients who, he knew, were far happier when they could put a name to whatever was ailing them. Shirley also knew he was a frustrated pathologist but had left it too late to change courses. That was why he so delighted in being one of the police surgeons. All right, mostly he was taking blood samples from drunk drivers, or examining victims of assault or rape, or reporting on the injuries of prisoners or policemen, but if he was available he turned up voluntarily at post-mortems.

Tonight Ian asked him only one question: would it have been possible for a woman to have manoeuvred the body into such a position that she could have then tipped it into the tunnel?

'It's only an opinion, Ian, but a woman could certainly have inflicted that head wound. Any metal object, swung at the right trajectory, or with enough hatred, would do the trick without a tremendous amount of strength. The other thing, though – unless she's amazingly strong, no, I doubt it. Why, do you have a suspect?'

'Over a hundred of them. Unfortunately, not one of them female. You were right, by the way. He was killed, then his body moved. We're now trying to find out where he had his last meal.'

'Important?'

'I'm convinced of it. Ah, talking of food, I think it's ready. One day I think we ought to buy a house with a dining-room.'

'I shouldn't bother. Your kitchen's cosy. We've got one and we never use it.'

Ian helped Moira clear up after their guests had left. 'Who was he, this man who was killed?' she asked.

'A miner originally. Similar sort of thing to what he was doing here.'

'I didn't mean that. I meant, what was he like?'

80

'Good-looking bloke, strong. Twice married, lots of kids, all the ex-family still very fond of him. The same at work, no one's got a word to say against him.'

'Girlfriend? Only I heard you say something to The Doc about a woman.'

'We don't know.'

'It would surprise me if he didn't have.'

'No one admits to seeing him with anyone.'

'Married, then.'

'Yes. Of course.' What Moira suggested was no great revelation. He and Barry had already discussed that aspect. A man of Daniels' age would be hard pushed to find many single females, especially if he did all his socialising in the rougher pubs of the town. There, it was quite likely he'd come across someone not too fussy, who was out on the town with a friend or possibly even with her husband. These things could always be arranged. But if she was married, say, and her husband was away, or worked shifts, or had gone into hospital to have his haemorrhoids removed, or whatever, then it was more than possible she had taken him home and cooked him a meal. She would not, after all, want to be seen in public places too often.

'What have I said?'

'Food for thought, that's all, love. What would you do under the circumstances?' Ian asked when he explained his theory.

'Oh, Ian, I wouldn't do such a thing.'

'I wasn't implying you would. But I mean, does it seem logical, is that what a woman might do?'

'Yes. Especially if she was more than keen. It forms a sort of bond, doesn't it, cooking someone a meal? It takes things one step further from just getting your leg over.'

'Moira!' Ian was always shocked when she came out with a phrase he considered to be crude. There was plenty of vulgarity at the station, it didn't shock him in that respect, nor was it because she was female. It was just that she was so dainty and blonde and angelic to look at, her uttering the words made them seem worse than they actually were.

'And talking of, well, that, now that Lucy's finally moved in with super-stud Swan, do you suppose they'll get married?'

'I think that's what he wants. Oh, God, I've just remembered. Where's Judy?'

'She went back to her flat this morning. She's got to arrange the funeral and everything, then decide what to do with her father's place. It's pretty run down, I believe. She left me a note and some flowers and said we weren't to worry.'

'I feel dreadful. I hadn't given her a thought all day.'

'You've got enough on your plate. I'll go and see her tomorrow.'

'Good. Come on, let's leave the rest. I'm shattered.'

Ian lay awake for quite a while. If his theory was right, and there was a married woman involved, however would they find her? If her husband didn't know about the affair and Daniels was now dead, there was no reason whatsoever for her to come forward. If her husband did know, of course, it was more than possible he'd killed him.

Just as he felt sleep creeping up on him he thought that she might not even live in Rickenham. This fictional irate husband might have waited until Daniels had moved safely out of his own area.

7

During the night the weather changed dramatically. Gale-force winds caused havoc to fences and loose tiles. Litter was swept skywards and occasionally became lodged in the bare branches of trees; Tesco carriers, tissues, bits of newspaper hung there like bizarre Christmas decorations after the needles have dropped. By dawn, seemingly satisfied with the damage, the high winds abated and it started to rain. Although it was not many degrees higher, the temperature seemed so because of the absence of sleet and snow.

For some reason, as he drove to work, Ian thought of summer holidays. This year he had promised to take Moira somewhere exotic with guaranteed sunshine. She would love every minute, while he'd be counting them until he could return home. 'Not true,' he told himself. 'I don't really hate holidays, I just don't enjoy them as much as her.' And there was no proper beer abroad.

There was some new graffiti on the bus station wall. He couldn't understand why anyone bothered to clean it off. Better to leave it until the whole damn thing was covered and no one could read any of it.

'Ah!' An idea had come to him out of the blue. 'France! That's where we'll go. Moira can have her sunshine and at least there'll be some decent wine.' The power of advertising was far greater than he believed. His subconscious had recorded the special offer sheets plastered all over the off-licence window.

'More information, sir,' Barry said once Ian had hung up his coat and flicked through his in-tray. 'Stomach contents analysis. Sounds like a typical Sunday lunch. Beef and vegetables and a fair amount of alcohol.'

'And that goes one step further to proving my theory.'

'I wasn't aware you had one.'

'No? Well, if – as I think is possible – Daniels was knocking off a married woman, it's also possible she cooked him a meal.'

'Plenty of pubs do food, Ian.' Back to Christian names now they were out of the earshot of other officers.

'Roast beef, et cetera? In the evenings? No, lunchtimes, maybe. And if he was with her, they wouldn't want to be seen in restaurants.'

'We don't know that he was. Perhaps he took himself out to eat, somewhere different for a change, away from the rest of them.'

'I just can't see it. Not knowing the type of man he was. I think it's worth looking into further. Someone is doing the rounds of the pubs?'

'Organised yesterday, if you remember.'

'There is, unfortunately, one other possibility. We know his car was in a different position from where he'd left it in the morning. Suppose he drove himself back there, cooked himself a meal in the canteen and then got killed – actually in the compound, I mean?'

'The timing's wrong. I can't imagine he sat there for a couple of hours after he ate.'

'No, I didn't mean that. He cooked something, ate, left his car there while he went for a couple of drinks – there was alcohol in the stomach contents and blood sample – he returned for his car, and, bingo. Come on, let's get the briefing over with.'

Jeremy Saunders smiled where most men would have torn their hair out. Perhaps it helped that he had very little of it, a few grey strands, brushed from just above one ear over the top of a shining dome. He thought, as he was spokesman for the Water Board, their public relations man, he ought to have a word with the local constabulary. Apart from the usual complaints, he was receiving what might amount to threatening calls – if he was the sort of man to take any notice, that is.

'No, I'm not in any danger, Sergeant Swan, it's just – I wondered, is it possible that you can reassure the public in any way? Not only am I inundated with complaints about the mess, the noise, the blasting and the general cost of the whole operation, but people are now getting paranoid, asking why it is we've allowed a murderer on the job.'

'We don't know that, sir. It might be a local person. I'll have to speak to my superintendent but it's another week until the *Herald* comes out. I really don't think there's a lot we can do.'

'Oh, well, thanks for listening. It'll stop when you catch him, I suppose.'

Jeremy hung up, not knowing how gratified Barry was by his total faith that they would catch Daniels' killer.

Jeremy took a few, slow sips of his coffee before he picked up the insistently ringing telephone again. Once the populace had realised the job involved blasting, it seemed that half the properties in Rickenham had suddenly acquired cracks in the walls and that the noise kept the occupiers awake all night. Most of them threatened to take it further. Whatever that meant. If it was not for the regulations which stated that a siren must sound a few minutes before each blast, none of them would have been any the wiser. As for keeping them awake at night, Jeremy found this rather odd as they hadn't started double-shifting yet, and those who claimed to hear it in the daytime must possess supersonic hearing. One old lady had rung eleven times. Her house must be uninhabitable as there were now, apparently, huge cracks in both walls and ceilings and all her crockery had been smashed with the force of the blasts. She had received three visits from an inspector who was offered a cup of tea and was tactful enough not to mention that her tea set and cups seemed to have escaped the blitz.

The lady in question would have been proud to know she had a file to herself. Jeremy knew she was lonely.

He was perfect for the job. He never took the complaints personally and his sense of humour never let him down. Later that morning came the best call of them all so far.

'Now, I do realise that this work has to go on,' said the voice at the other end with a pronounced Suffolk burr, 'but you see, I believe in total health. I don't drink or smoke, and I never eat any foods with additives.' Jeremy wondered what on earth she did eat if this was the case. 'I have a very strict regime, you see, and I drink the required amount of water every day. But tell me, young man, how can I possibly do this when my tap water's contaminated with dead bodies? I shall, of course, write to the Ombudsman.'

While he explained the situation, Jeremy held back his laughter as his mind conjured up a picture of corpses trying to burst through domestic water taps throughout the area.

Tomorrow would bring more problems. The local television station was sending reporters and cameramen. It was a propaganda exercise: the public liked to see where their money was going. No doubt the press would manage to get in everyone's way while they were at it. The *Rickenham Herald* was doing a similar exercise in a few days. Martyn Bright, the editor, was more than pleased. He scraped around for news most weeks, but now, with a murder to add to it, no man could be happier.

'What did he want?' Ian asked.

'He wanted to know if we could reassure the public that it's not the Water Board's policy to employ serial killers.'

'Great. I hope you said no.'

'More or less.'

'Okay. Everyone's aware that we need to know where the victim ate his last meal.'

'A bit like the Last Supper.'

'Thank you, Emmanuel, I'd prefer you listened rather than made feeble attempts at humour. It seems a waste of manpower to send someone to every pub and restaurant in the vicinity. Anyone got any ideas?'

'Yes, sir,' DC Winston Emmanuel volunteered. He was rewarded with a raised eyebrow. The Chief must think he was about to get smart.

As he listened to what was said, Ian nodded. It was a very good idea.

Operation Keyring had been under way for several months. No one enjoyed working on it particularly; it was unlike a drugs ring or a post office or bank raid where there was something to get your teeth into. A directive had come down from regional headquarters. There was to be a clamp-down on the rapidly rising crime of car theft. It was understood that most of these offences were committed by youths, and these youths seemed to be getting younger by the minute, learning their trade from those who had stepped their activities up a notch. The general idea was to target the criminals rather than investigating each incident separately, thus saving time and money. By the time the theft was reported and someone had attended the scene, the culprit and the car had disappeared but the paperwork still had to be done.

The success of the new approach was yet to be judged officially but the figures in Rickenham showed an improvement. However, the officers occasionally felt a little ridiculous when they were posted to overlook a certain car-park which was a popular target, perched in the branches of a tree. Fortunately, now that winter was upon them, their viewing points had altered. If they saw a crime they radioed the nearest patrol car with the details. This way several arrests had been made.

The directive had suggested that prevention was better than detection but the roles of the men involved overlapped. Detection was down to CID, prevention to the men on the beat. As it was likely that the title of detective was to be dropped and that briefings would be joint affairs, now seemed as good a time as any to begin the interchange of roles.

'The prevention side, sir,' Winston continued, 'is going quite well. The flatfoots are visiting all public places and advising on lighting and video cameras and alarm systems, and the *Herald*'s going to run a piece on personal security, marking items, that sort of thing. Whilst they're at it, going round the pubs, et cetera, why don't they make the inquiries about Daniels at the same time?'

'Why not indeed? Very good suggestion. How's it going, by the way?'

'Quite well. Several incidents where youths have owned up to more than one offence. One lad's claimed responsibility for a list as long as your arm. The problem is –'

'Don't remind me. I know what the problem is, he'll get a pat on the bottom and be told not to be a naughty boy. All right, Emmanuel, I'll leave it to you to have a word with the duty sergeant.'

It turned out to be one of those days when nothing was achieved. No further leads came in and there seemed little option but to go home.

Barry said Lucy was going to the cinema with a girl-friend. 'Oh, some arty film, French I think, with subtitles. Not my cup of tea.'

'Nor mine,' Ian admitted. 'All those long silences and crashing waves and trains rushing into tunnels. Oh, God. Why did I say that? Can't get away from the bloody things. Come on, you can buy me a drink.'

'Jesus.' They knew it was raining but until they left the building they were not aware of the force of it. Rain hammered off the roofs of cars and cascaded down the pipes from the gutters. Water gushed into drains and splashed from the kerb as traffic passed by. 'I think we'd better go in my car,' Barry said.

They did so, Ian remembering the one time he had accompanied Moira to a foreign film. One of their 'discussions' had followed, which ended with Ian commenting strongly on the sad loss of the British film industry and Moira tartly retaliating by saying she was too young to remember it.

Despite the elements there were several customers enjoying the warmth of the fires, the beer and an hour's convivial conversation before they went home to their wives or an empty house. A delicious aroma of lamb and garlic reached them from the kitchen regions.

'Evening, Bob. Usual, and – Barry?'

'Lager, please.'

'What's Connie making you tonight? Smells wonderful.'

Bob Jones shook his head. 'I know it does. That's for the customers, tomorrow lunchtime. It'll be something straight from the freezer to the microwave for me.'

Ian gulped back the first few inches of Adnams, his second true love after Moira. 'Mm ... That reminds me, do many of the pubs do evening meals, proper cooked ones, I mean, not sandwiches or something with chips?'

'I would've thought you'd know that better than anyone, Ian, old chap, knowing your inclination for the odd pint or two.'

'I can get insulted in the Feathers, thank you.'

'Serious question? We do a special occasionally, as you know. Theme food, Connie calls it. Either Italian or Mexican or whatever. We've got to get the money in somehow. Apart from that we only do lunchtimes. You'd never stop otherwise. I think most governors feel the same. Put on a good menu midday then offer a few basics at night. Work, is it?'

'Yes. What about round the villages?'

'Much the same. We all tend to know what everyone else is doing, it's the only way to keep up. And we get together at brewery meetings.'

'No one you know does an evening roast then?'

'Nope. Not round here.' Bob folded his arms across a stomach which was a good advertisement for his bitter or his wife's cooking, or both.

Barry's glass was empty. 'Your turn,' Ian said. When they each had a refill they went to a table near the door. There was a not unpleasant smell of wet clothing emanating from the coat rack. 'It's looking more like a private house, isn't it?'

'But where would he have met her? And if you're right, and I'm beginning to think you are, how come none of his mates knew about it? Surely it's the sort of thing to warrant a mention, if not to boast about.'

At that point Ian disagreed. He had never boasted about any female conquests, not that there had been any since he married Moira, although he'd had his chances like anyone else. The same with his wife. He was immensely proud of her looks and her abilities but he rarely spoke of her at work. 'God, I don't know. Perhaps there's more to it all than meets the eye. Look, all those men, and what've we turned up? A couple of men claiming travelling expenses to which they're not entitled; that bloke Kavanagh living half illegally on the site; one lost licence due to drink/driving – again, don't you think that amongst all those men someone must've done something? It all seems too good to be true.'

'You mean a mass conspiracy? I hardly think it's likely. No, same old story, if you ask me. *Cherchez la femme.*'

Ian grinned. 'You picked that phrase up from Judy Robbins.'

'I know. How is she?'

'She'll survive. She was very pleased you called round, you know. I don't suppose she'll tell you so herself.'

'I'm glad,' Barry said, lighting a cigarette to cover his embarrassment.

Marie Dixon was on edge. She did not want it to be time for Phil to go but she wanted to get the assignation with Neil Thomas out of the way. She was a little wary of his reaction. She hardly knew him. She guessed that he was frightened of his wife, which was enough to ensure he didn't start making a fuss, but there was the slight possibility he might become violent. Unfortunately she had just read a book where, in a similar situation, the man committed murder, and this did little for the state of her mind. She was distracted and unsettled and did not notice Nichola's long periods of silence. All she could do was wait.

That night, as it was Saturday, Kate went to stay with her grandmother so Phil could take his wife out. Nichola was also out, but was due back on the last bus, from which she'd go immediately to join her sister. The Dixons were not worried. Kate and Nichola were good kids.

Phil dropped Nichola off in the town centre, outside the cinema, where she was ostensibly meeting Sally. Her father watched as she entered the foyer, fumbling in her bag for her purse. Nichola waited five minutes, then walked out again.

It was a nuisance, having to be on that last bus, but there was no way she was going to jeopardise her future. She knew she was not like other people; already she had made up her mind she wanted everything. Going with men and drinking, for instance – it was almost as if she wanted to get all that out of the way before going to university. There was another aspect: escape from what she felt was the tedious boredom of her parents' lives. 'But I have jeopardised it all already,' she acknowledged as she made her way to Debbie's. They'd be safe tonight. Debbie's mother didn't finish until after midnight and Debbie had promised to make some inquiries for her.

Paul and Wayne were already there and had brought the necessary bottle of vodka and some mixers. Debbie provided a few packets of crisps and some nuts and a litre of cider in case the vodka ran out.

'Hello, gorgeous,' Paul said, kissing Nicky on the cheek. He put a possessive arm around her shoulders, wishing that her parents weren't so strict and that he could be seen in public with her. He had never expected to meet anyone like her. Usually, after a disco, say, he ended up with a girl no one else wanted. Nicky was slim and beautiful and clever and Paul had never experienced half the emotions he was now capable of until he met her. Looking at her made his loins ache, being with her made him happy. If she was quiet and he believed he'd upset her, he sank into depths of misery he did not know existed. And there was something else. She was so modest. Paul knew from Debbie that Nicky would probably get a place at a university yet not once had she mentioned it. That was typical. She was too kind to want to make him feel inferior. He would wait or, better still, get a job in whichever town or city she went to. He was a good worker and didn't mind what he did. His appearance belied his strength. He'd always done manual work but had never filled out like his brother. His prominent cheekbones made him look thinner. 'Drink?'

'Please,' Nicky said, following him into the lounge. She asked a silent question of Debbie, who winked. Nicky immediately relaxed and threw herself into the evening.

'Are you all right?' she asked Paul some time later.

'Of course I am if I'm with you. Why?'

'You're shaking.'

'See what you do to me.'

Nicky smiled. She was aware that Paul would do anything for her, anything at all. Right now she was tempted to ask him for the one thing she really needed. There were two reasons why this was not possible. First, it would put

92

her under an obligation. Second, and more important, if she did, he would know.

She and Debbie went out to the kitchen to make some toast and coffee before Nichola caught the bus.

'Well?' Nicky said.

'This is what you need to do.'

'I see,' Nicky replied when Debbie had told her the score. There was, however, another possibility which crossed her mind as she stood at the bus stop, oblivious to the rain which was falling in a steady shower and plastering her long, dark hair to her head.

Ian was always glad when he had to go in on a Sunday. This was no reflection on his family and he knew he must, before it was too late, take up some hobby. When it was fine he and Moira and Mark, though Mark hardly ever joined them now, went out somewhere and had a walk and a couple of drinks or sat in the sun. In the winter they tended to waste the day. Ian knew it was his fault. He'd eat his meal and slump in front of the television watching football. At this point Mark either retired to his room or went out, and Moira went upstairs to read or sew.

Today, however, he had to go in. They got up late, about nine thirty. Moira made coffee and ignored Ian's complaints that he needed the lavatory and what the bloody hell was Mark doing in there.

'Imagine what it would be like if we had a daughter.'

'It couldn't be worse. Have you seen all the stuff he's got up there? Deodorant and aftershave and God knows what else.'

'Yes, Ian. I have seen it. I'm the one who cleans the bathroom and I don't need to hear how in your day a weekly scrub in the tin bath with carbolic or a hose down with Lysol was enough.'

'You really are a bitch sometimes, Moira.'

'Yes,' she said sweetly. 'I know.'

'Problem, sir?' the duty sergeant asked as Ian rushed past him and took the stairs two at a time. He received no reply.

Having used the station lavatory, Ian washed his hands and ran a hand through his hair as he leant forward to peer in the mirror. He was tired and it made him irritable. Why couldn't anyone understand that?

What on earth he hoped to achieve today was beyond him. At least Barry Swan was coming in as well.

Neil Thomas was counting the hours until he could see Marie again. First he had to survive another Sunday and its abysmal routine.

He was beginning to recognise the signs of guilt, not because of his affair, but because of that argument. Was he mistaken? Had he misheard? No, there was nothing wrong with his hearing. It unnerved him, knowing that someone may have heard him threaten to kill Daniels, but if they had, why wasn't he under arrest?

'No,' he said, 'no, no. I must stop this. It's driving me mad.'

Eleven o'clock. Any second the phone would ring. A duty call from Martin. Why did he bother when he knew they had nothing in common? 'For his mother's sake, I suppose,' he added, 'because as long as he rings, she can make believe we're one happy family, and a lucky one at that, to have such a fine, talented son.'

'Hello, darling,' Marg said. 'How's city life?' Neil could have written the script for the conversation. It never varied. Finally, 'Do you want a quick word with Dad?' Marg handed him the receiver and he went through the formalities. Martin had scraped into college but had some-how found his niche – once he was over the embarrassment of his parents going to London with him and escorting him to both the college and his digs. He had never looked back. He was a genius with computers and was earning a fortune. Now married to an ex-model, he had two small children.

'It was only a registry office do,' Martin had explained when he telephoned to say he was married. 'We didn't want any fuss. It's not like that down here.' Later, Neil learned they'd had thirty guests – the maximum number permitted – at the wedding: his wife's family and his college friends. Thank goodness Marg didn't know. They had seen their grandchildren twice.

In a way, Neil understood his son's reluctance in this respect. He knew himself how people stared at Marg when they were out together. It wasn't even that people were being unkind – she was so enormous you couldn't help but look.

Marie had two daughters whom he had not met and had no desire to meet. It was Marie he wanted.

For now he must content himself with the enormous midday meal which would be on the table at twelve thirty, the washing and drying of dishes, then a couple of hours with the Sunday paper. Tonight, whether she wanted to go or not, he was determined to take Marg to the pub. He could not bear the thought of four hours of mindless television viewing.

'Are you all right?' Marg asked him. 'You're very quiet.'

'Problems at work,' Neil said. A safe answer. Marg had no idea what he actually did.

'You're right there, you are, Tony. It'll be another Guinness you'll be after having?'

Tony nodded. He had strung together two sentences and didn't think he could cope with a third.

'And you say you heard yer man? You should've told the police.'

Tony shrugged.

'Ah, I see what you mean,' Paddy Malone wisely concurred. Tony would not have been able to sustain a conversation. All right, he might have written down what he wanted to say, but there were other considerations, like not dropping your workmates in it, and Gerry Daniels was a good workmate. They had been with him three years ago, and this time had ended up sharing the same room. Certain things were better left unsaid, although Tony had almost blurted it out to Markham. And there was that other little business, back home in Ireland. Long ago, but not, he was sure, forgotten.

In the end he might as well have spoken, for the evening took an unusual turn.

The Plough, on a Sunday night, attracted a different clientele, that is, even rougher than usual. Tonight was someone's birthday or stag night, it didn't matter which. All that did matter was that a strippergram had been arranged. At ten o'clock, when the girl arrived, the bar was full. At first no one took much notice when a youngish female, averagely attractive, but by no means beautiful, asked Brian Greenham, the landlord, who a particular person was.

Colin Jordan noticed this exchange and thought little of it. He had persuaded Tom Clancey to join him there for a drink. The disparities in their characters and their domestic situations seemed not to matter. Basically they held the same principles and beliefs. In another walk of life they might have ignored each other. Situated as they were, two natural loners, they were company.

Tom was married with three children and a mortgage. His wife was a hairdresser; his children, he said, were mostly a pain in the neck. Colin sensed from these words that he was happy. Colin was single and always had been. He guessed he always would be. Yet he lived and planned his life as if one day there would be someone to share it. He had bought a bungalow in Devon where he spent his holidays and tried to get to know the locals. It was, he told himself, also an investment, for his old age. There were, barring accidents, another fourteen years to get through before he retired and lived there full time. But what then? Would he sit there, television on, waiting for death?

'Let's have another,' he offered, in an attempt to divert his thoughts. Before they could order it they saw that most of the customers had congregated in one corner of the bar.

The girl employed to do the strippergram was nervous and obviously doing it to supplement her income. She was not a natural and had no idea how to deal with the comments she was receiving. Perhaps she was used to more salubrious venues.

Colin and Tom turned to see what all the fuss was about, shrugged, smiled and turned back to more serious matters like getting a drink: they had seen it all before and not much was likely to happen in a public bar on a Sunday night.

Paddy and Tony Malone had a different view of the situation. Brought up in a family with strong moral views and educated by Christian brothers, they had a black and white outlook on life. Women fell into two categories: saints or whores. The student nurse, unsuccessfully trying to build up a sideline, obviously fell into the latter category.

They turned their backs.

Tony and Paddy did not see any discrepancies in their beliefs. Some of the things they had done in their lives were not exactly commendable.

The ratio of cheering and comments increased in proportion to the amount of discarded clothing. The man for whom this display was intended was drunk and started to remove his own clothing in the belief that he was going to get a lot more than would be provided by the fifty pounds his friends had clubbed together and raised.

Brian Greenham grinned. He would have to stop it if things went too far. At the moment they were still within the limits of decency. Paddy Malone did not agree. The expression on the girl's face as the man tried to maul her told him all he needed to know. The crowd were going along with it, egging him on, shouting louder.

'That's enough, lads,' Paddy said quietly but with enough menace for notice to be taken as he pushed through the gathered men.

'Mind your own business,' someone said aggressively. 'We've paid for her, we'll do what we like.'

Paddy took one more look at the girl. Her eyes were full of pleading. The man for whose benefit all this had been arranged was gripping her upper arm.

'She's done her act, let her go.' Paddy was no stranger to pubs; he'd been in rougher ones than this and lived to tell the tale. His instinct told him the punch was coming. He ducked and bent sideways, clasping a wrist in his strong, workworn hand. His grip was like steel and the man winced. 'Let her go . . .' but there was nothing more he could do. Three of them had jumped him. Out of one eye he saw a streak of bare flesh and knew the girl had got away. It didn't matter what happened to him now, he had achieved his ends.

He was too intent on defending himself to realise that Tony had joined in the fray. As his mission was accomplished he threw himself wholeheartedly into the battle. It was a long time since he'd enjoyed a decent fight.

Some time later, minutes or longer, he was aware of space all around him. From his semi-prone position he had no need to look further than the highly polished black shoes and the serge trouser bottoms. It would not be the first time he had been taken in for questioning: it went with the job. It was infuriating, but understandable. Paddy held no political views himself, but he and Tony were itinerant workers, Irish, and they dealt with explosives. A lethal combination. He saw how it might appear. They were cleared, of course, both of them, to be able to use the drill and blast method. This was a different matter.

They had been involved in a pub brawl on someone else's territory. He did not think an explanation of self-defence would get him very far.

He had not counted on the landlord. Brian Greenham had not witnessed the entire episode, but he said it was not the Malones' fault. Whether it was or not was irrelevant. The important thing was that they and The Goat had paid for their accommodation in advance and spent more in a week in the bar than all the rest of his customers put together – apart from the friends they also brought in. The brewery were ecstatic. The two months following Christmas were usually a waste of time.

The two patrol officers who had come in response to the call took everyone's details, gave them all a warning and left it at that. They would, however, run a check on the Malones. If what they said was true they might have known the recently murdered man. The officers were not aware that they had already been questioned and that they had actually shared a room with Daniels.

Paddy leant against the bar, grinning at the sight of his brother. Tony's red hair stood on end, his lip was cut and he was clutching his ribs.

'You d-d-don't look g-good yourself.'

Many of the customers had left at the first sign of trouble, Colin Jordan and Tom Clancey amongst them. They'd been around too long to want to get involved.

'I think we'd better have another one, isn't that right, Tony, for medicinal purposes.'

Tony nodded.

'This one's on me,' Greenham said. The brothers stared at each other in astonishment as soon as his back was turned.

Nichola Dixon had spent Sunday afternoon round at Sally's. Genuinely. They did their homework together. As she made her way to the bus stop in time for the seven forty-five, she passed Tom and Colin going in the opposite direction on their way to the Plough. She was near enough to have touched them. But she didn't know them and they did not know her. Had they done so, things might have been different.

'It's not possible,' Ian said into the receiver. 'Oh, God, I'll have to come in.'

'I heard,' Moira said, resting her book on her knees. 'If you're late, make sure Mark's in first before you put the chain on. He's gone into Ipswich with Tina and he said he'd be late.' He had been taking driving lessons, supplemented by his mother's coaching. She was not a nervous passenger but it was a strange experience being driven by her son. Mark was amazingly confident although she thought he drove too fast. At least for the moment she did not have to wait up, worrying that he had written the car off and himself with it.

'He hasn't got the car, has he?'

'No. Calm down. You know he hasn't.'

'Sorry. I was looking forward to a quiet evening in.'

After he left Moira decided they must discuss getting a second car. It would be a ridiculous situation if three of them were to share the same one. Maybe one of the men at work would know where to get a reliable banger.

The PCs on patrol duty in the area of the Plough were Jackson and Stone. They were conscientious men and mostly enjoyed their work. Their relationship was a strange one, considering the twenty-two-year difference in their ages. Frank Stone was the senior, in years, not rank, yet there were occasions when Jackson seemed almost to mother him. PC Stone did not hanker back to the good old days, as they were euphemistically called by some of his colleagues. He had no desire whatsoever to walk the streets of a much enlarged Rickenham Green, day or night, depending on the shift, and in all weathers. Much nicer to be warm in the car, and it was quicker and better equipped for communication. He could still be fast when he needed to be and as the years went by his increased mental agility made up for any decline in other directions. And if his wife complained about the extra weight he carried, it did not unduly worry him.

Pub fights were common to him. He and Jackson had broken this one up and used their judgement. No point in senseless paperwork when it would all be forgotten in the morning. It was not like some East End vendetta.

Stone reported to the control room and suggested a check on the Malone brothers. It was a chance in a million, but not one to be overlooked.

The routine of a murder inquiry was well under way. Squad numbers 1 and 2 on house-to-house had completed their task and now squad number 3 came into its own, following up on all information available.

On this new information received from PC Stone, being already aware that the two men were not local and of their daily, or, rather, nightly, proximity to Gerry Daniels, they bypassed the Regional Criminal Intelligence Offices and went straight to the NIB. The National Identification Bureau had replaced the old Criminal Records Office.

The name Patrick Anthony Malone showed up on the screen.

Number 3 squad requested all details to be faxed as quickly as possible. The Chief arrived not long after this request had been made.

'Christ Almighty, this can't be happening. Not here.' He was almost praying as other agencies went to work.

Superintendent Thorne saw fit to leave his wife at their friends' house where they had been enjoying a meal.

'Don't worry,' she said. 'I'll get a cab if you don't come back.'

At least he was in slacks and a jacket. On one occasion he'd had to leave a formal dinner and felt a bit of a fool in his penguin suit. Until he'd slipped off the jacket and removed his bow-tie he felt incapable of handling the situation, which was ridiculous for a man in his position. Which just goes to show, he thought when his driver collected him, how clothes can affect behaviour. In his career he had come across two people who, once inside their uniform, changed from ordinary and sensible blokes into men with a power complex. Their uniforms had soon been taken away.

It spoke volumes for Roper's man management that the wheels were turning smoothly without Roper having to start the ignition himself. Each man under him had acted precisely as they should before ringing him at home.

'My mistake. It was one aspect I didn't look into.'

It was typical he chose to blame no one else. 'No reason why you should have, Ian. Nelson Enterprises must have checked them out. Don't I remember you telling me they did? Anything come through yet?' Thorne asked.

'No. Too soon. And we can't get hold of Harrington – apparently he's gone home for the weekend. He's not in. I've left a message on his answering machine.'

The atmosphere at HQ was completely different at night. The building seemed larger, and hollow, with fewer staff and less bustle. With most of the offices unlit it also seemed unfriendly. A sort of dry, dusty heat circulating from the radiators predominated, compared with the early-morning smell of the antiseptic the cleaners used in their mopping up, and there was an aura of damp clothing. It had stopped raining, which was about the best that could be said for the evening.

'Can I get you some coffee, Mike?'

'Love one. Not much of a substitution for salmon *en croute* and a drop of wine, but it'll have to do.'

Before he could organise it, the external line rang. Ian answered it.

'Yes, it is. Thank you for calling us back. You're absolutely positive?' he said after a long pause. 'I'm very pleased to hear it.'

'I can imagine what you've been thinking. They get used to it, believe me,' Harrington told him before he hung up.

'Does this mean I can return to the salmon?'

'Looks that way. Turned out to be nothing. Paddy Malone was pulled for speeding on the M1. Traffic, for whatever reasons, searched the car . . .'

'Don't tell me, explosives.'

'No. Detonators. He shouldn't have had them on him – he was doing his boss a favour. Poor sod spent a lot of hours being questioned over that one. Sorry to have dragged you out.'

'It had to be checked. All the ingredients were there, unlikely though it seems, especially with the victim and the Malones being of different religions.'

Ian shook his head. 'No. I think we all panicked. It was an easy solution but we didn't consider the method of his dying. No terrorist of any description would go about removing someone in that manner.'

'For goodness sake, Ian, don't look so glum. You did the right thing. Supposing it had been that and you'd failed to see it . . .'

'I did fail to see it. It was a couple of PCs who thought it ought to be checked because the Malones were involved in a pub fight.'

'Go home yourself, Ian. There's no point in hanging around getting morose.'

'I'll just wait to see what the NIB has to say.'

'Please yourself. I'm off.'

Thorne went on his way. Ian was surprised to note that, although he was so smartly dressed in every other way, he pulled a red woollen scarf from the pocket of his raincoat and tied it, Rupert Bear fashion, around his neck. He also wondered whether it was possible to purchase a good winter coat any more. Everyone he knew seemed to favour macs.

'I felt such a damn fool,' he told Moira, who was struggling to keep her eyes open. 'We alerted everyone, including MI5.'

'Forget it, Ian. You did the right thing. Now, if you don't mind, I'd like to go back to sleep.'

'So much for sympathy,' he muttered to himself as he crept downstairs. Mark was in, he had remembered to check.

He was on his second scotch before he realised that it was number 3 squad, not himself, who had initiated things and that, had they not done so, he would have screamed blue murder.

The mood was not good at the compound on Monday morning. Tempers were frayed, and not only because some of the men were nursing hangovers. There was an air of suspicion which had been slowly developing over the past few days. Each of them was becoming more convinced that Gerry Daniels had died at the hands of one of their own number. They were all watching their backs.

'Look out!' Alastair Menzies shouted as the morning drew to a close. Three of them were standing at the base of the shaft when the man-rider began to swing erratically. They were not really in any danger and no one was in it at the time, but it shouldn't have happened, especially as the air above was still. Normally Alastair would not have reacted so violently. It showed the state of his nerves.

Colin, sitting at the controls of the crane, swore softly. He had momentarily lost concentration. He had been thinking about something he overheard Tony say last night in the Plough before the fight started. Except, with

Tony, it wasn't always clear what he meant. Only his brother understood him fully. When he couldn't get the words right, he substituted others, like a code used between the two of them. Added to what Tom had said he overheard, it was not putting Gerry Daniels in such a good light.

There would be further dissatisfaction if the men knew all their names had been given to the National Identification Bureau.

The idea had come to Ian, as did most of his good ideas, just before he fell asleep. Jack Harrington had told him that any past misdemeanours or criminal activities would show up on their files. Paddy Malone's hadn't, yet Harrington had known about it. How many other similar incidents might there be? And the jobs were all obtained by word of mouth. Ian was pretty sure that as long as these employees did the job – got the tunnel built, caulked and sealed within the stipulated period – no one would care if they had a record as long as your arm. And those not actually handling the explosives did not need a licence.

They did ascertain a few more facts and figures during that Monday, but nothing which helped pinpoint Gerry Daniels' killer.

There had been other arrests for breach of the peace, causing a public disturbance, and a couple of grievous bodily harms. No one had been arrested on suspicion of murder. Which didn't mean none of them were capable of it.

A few more forensic results dribbled in from the lab but proved nothing.

'I hate all this waiting around, but for the life of me I can't think where we ought to look next.'

'Don't be so glum,' Barry told him. 'You know you always go through this phase.'

'And what's that supposed to mean?'

'At this stage, when we reach an impasse – it almost always happens. Why don't we go out and get something to eat? I'm sick of the food in the canteen. I'll even buy you a pint to go with it. And anyway, you've often told me the waiting's an important part.'

'Have I? Mm, I can smell curry, I think.' Strange how happy the thought of food could make the Chief.

'Yes. You know, wait long enough and someone'll make a mistake.'

It was true. How often did someone think they'd got away with a crime and then have to boast about it to prove it? There was a small minority who were not interested in the crime *per se* but in the publicity or notoriety awarded them for their exploits. It was not unknown for the police to be contacted and given hints and suggestions by the villain himself.

'I think we might ask Brian Lord for some advice.'

'Any port in a storm, I suppose.' Barry did not share Ian's regard for the police psychologist. Ian had started respecting him only once he realised that Lord talked sense regarding the stress experienced by police officers and that he did not believe all crime could be put down to a deprived – whatever that meant – youth. Also, and here they agreed wholeheartedly, he believed some people were simply born bad.

Brian Lord himself was not totally conversant with his role. He counselled men, interviewed suspects if it was felt necessary, and did his best to 'profile' suspects, although, at times, it was beyond him how he was supposed to draw a mental picture of someone unknown to him. He surprised himself more than anyone else when he was close to the mark.

'I wish Moira'd never got you on to this,' Barry declared when Ian made it clear he was prepared to eat a curry and nothing else. 'I was talking about a couple of pints and a ham roll.'

'You shouldn't've offered, then. Seriously, I know you don't like Brian, but it's another head.'

Brian was available at three thirty that afternoon as he had no classes until the evening. 'Can you see anything we're missing?' Ian asked. Surreptitiously, or so he thought, he turned to lift the window a couple of inches, not caring that it was only four degrees above freezing.

Brian grinned. 'Is my pipe bothering you?'

'No, no. Carry on.' Barry, seated alongside the psychologist, nodded knowingly. Reformed characters were the least tolerant of others. Ian had once smoked a pipe.

'Well, for a start, it's virtually impossible for a man to be totally liked by everyone he comes into contact with. Virtually impossible, but I'm not saying it's out of the question. None of us has personally met this Gerry Daniels and I, for one, don't know enough about his background other than what you've told me. But yes, there must be something you've missed. Think about it.'

Ian shook his head. He didn't see where this was getting them.

'You've interviewed, what, seventy or more men. Far more, I imagine, than is normal. You've pointed out the inconsistency yourself.' He waved the stem of his pipe in Ian's direction as he spoke. A murky cloud of smoke drifted across. Ian blinked and coughed.

'Ah, I see what you're getting at. We'd already thought of it, though.'

'Yes,' Barry interrupted. 'No matter how respectable and law-abiding a murder victim might be, there's always somebody ready to make people think otherwise.'

'Precisely. And in this case you say no one's got anything but good to say of the man.' Brian leant back in his chair and ran a hand through his swept-back hair, which was overlong and streaked with grey. 'Now that, surely, has to be the pivot on which the case rests. Someone's covering for him in my opinion; over what? Your guess is as good as mine. If I knew what the murder weapon was I might have something to work on.'

'We don't know. Something heavy and metallic.'

'There you are, probably a man. That's a start.'

'Why do you say that?'

'Women don't usually take chances like that. They know men are stronger and that the weapon could be turned on themselves. If they wanted it that way, they'd get someone else to do it. They have more subtle methods. I did some research once; it showed women are great poisoners, men hardly ever are. Can I take these notes?'

Barry handed him a sheet of paper on which were handwritten notes concerning the life of Gerry Daniels. The rest of the information remained confidential.

'Do you know what I feel like doing?' Ian said when Brian left them. 'Just getting my head down and going to sleep.'

'Serves you right for overeating.'

8

It was not the first time it had happened, but it was unusual. A fight broke out in the tunnel. It meant immediate sacking for those involved. Alastair Menzies, as lead miner, understood the circumstances which had brought this fight about and was prepared to say nothing. However, one of the men had received a broken nose and a cut lip. All injuries, no matter how insignificant, had to be put in the daily report written by the Clerk of Works. Not only did the bosses need to know who was likely to be volatile, but Health and Safety regulations demanded it.

There would be no inquiry, no lengthy discussions. Fighting in the tunnel was forbidden.

The two men, and Alastair, went up in the man-rider. One walked straight to the drying room, changed, picked up his bags and left the compound. The second man, the injured party, believed he might get away with it. He was wrong.

Neil Thomas and the Clerk of Works were both in the office. They made one telephone call to Jack Harrington. Neil shook his head. 'Sorry, but you know the rules. It doesn't matter who started it, or why. Good luck.'

'What was it all about?' Harrington wanted to know later that day.

'I don't know,' Neil said. 'It happens.' But he did know.

It had started because the first man had said Gerry Daniels was knocking off a married woman out at Frampton, the very same one that he, Neil, was supposed to be seeing. The second man said that it was no such thing, that he knew exactly what was going on. He'd seen Gerry's bit of stuff, didn't she walk along outside the compound, very slowly, in the hope of seeing him? And then he explained who she was and what she was. It was then that he received his injuries. Gerry would not do that.

Thomas had listened to the man, dismissed his words with a wave of the hand and sent him packing. How he stopped himself shaking he didn't know. The thought, the very idea that the men believed Marie was that sort of woman made him sick. He picked up the telephone, he needed to hear her voice. He replaced it. He was seeing her tonight and he had promised not to ring. Besides, her husband might still be there.

Detective Chief Inspector Roper would have been more than interested to learn of these developments: they contained the vital clue.

Marie Dixon had got out of her warm bed at five fifteen that Monday morning. She had made her husband a mug of tea and some toast and, whilst he ate, she buttered four slices of bread and made a cheese and pickle and a ham salad and mustard sandwich for the first part of his journey.

Fifteen minutes earlier he had made love to her; briefly and perfunctorily, but it was as if he sensed something was wrong, or was tense himself. That might be it. This journey would take him near one of the trouble spots in Europe. She could not help feeling that their coupling was reminiscent of a cat spraying its territory, ensuring no other feline would go there. It was so unlike Phil's normal gentleness. But it was too late. Tonight, whatever happened, she would end whatever it was between herself and Neil.

When the front door closed she went back to bed and slept for an hour. Her daughters' breakfast out of the way, she watched them walk to the end of the road, muffled up against the cold, to wait for the bus. There was washing and housework to do, the lunchtime shift in the pub, Nicky and Kate back from school to be fed, then it would be over.

Her mother had looked at her suspiciously last time she asked her to keep an eye on the girls. Tonight it would not be necessary. They would be all right on their own for a couple of hours. She'd be back by eight. And tomorrow she would do what she'd been putting off. She would have a quiet chat with Nicky.

'I'm just popping up to see Val,' Marie said at six. A plate of home-made burgers, chips and peas was in front of each of her daughters. Marie's conscience would not allow her to throw together a sketchy meal from the freezer.

She walked up the road, in the direction of Val's house, which was the right direction in any case. Through the darkness, parked on the verge beneath some trees, she saw Neil's car. The lights were extinguished.

'Hello,' he said as he leaned across and opened the door for her. Immediately he started the engine and a warm blast from the heater wrapped itself around her feet. 'Where shall we go?'

'Oh, anywhere. I don't mind.'

'Are you all right, Marie?' Neil wanted to look at her face but he dared not. He pulled away immediately to lessen the risk of being seen. The road was narrow and twisting and unlit. An accident now would ruin everything.

'Do you want to go for a drink?'

'We can't, you know that.'

'There are places out of the way and no one goes out much in this weather.'

'No, Neil. I need to talk to you. Just park somewhere, would you?'

He was worried now. From the tone of her voice he guessed what she might want to tell him.

Seven miles outside Frampton he stopped under some trees, in a small clearing a little way off the road. He could only hope the tyres would get them out of there. The ground was muddy but not as bad as it had been. 'I've missed you, Marie – you don't know how much.'

'I've got to – ' but before she could continue Neil had cupped her face in his hands and was kissing her. Marie felt herself responding. Tonight Neil was more passionate than usual. He was always so caring and gentle, now he was on fire. Her brain told her it must stop, she had to finish it. Her body acted of its own volition, her hands already removing some of her clothing.

Neil reached under the passenger seat and released the catch that slid the seat back. In one swift movement he then lowered the seat back. He was on top of her, her hands in his hair, as she moaned with pleasure.

By the time he dropped her back in Frampton she knew she wanted it to last a little longer. He was not the type of man to whom she'd normally be attracted but once he touched her nothing else seemed to matter. She had not said a word about ending the affair.

Neil returned to his bungalow and Marg and only with great difficulty acted as if nothing had happened.

'Are you able to eat? How's the tooth?' she inquired as she laid the table for their evening meal. 'A bit late tonight, but it's stew so it doesn't matter.' In that moment he hated her with her talk of food and timetables, and her obesity only served to emphasise Marie's slimness.

'The tooth's fine,' he said, pulling back the side of his mouth with a forefinger to show her the non-existent filling which was his excuse for being late. He had telephoned to say an emergency dentist could see him at seven fifteen and that it wasn't worth driving back from Rickenham first.

When they went to bed Marg mercifully fell asleep immediately. Neil lay on his back, hands clasped behind his head, unable to believe how it had been that night. There was no doubt now: Marie was all his.

Only on Tuesday morning did Marg realise her husband must have collected the car some time during Monday. She had spent the latter part of the afternoon pushing a trolley around Safeway's then lugging three carrier bags back home on the bus, not an easy chore for a woman of her dimensions. If Neil had been hanging around the office for an hour, he could have utilised that time by giving her a lift with the stuff. There was a time when they had each had a car but Marg had found it increasingly difficult to fit behind the steering wheel and it was almost impossible to turn around in order to reverse. They had sold both cars and spent the money on a larger, better model.

She would challenge him with it later, after work. It wasn't fair to send him off in a bad mood, especially with the pressure he was under at the moment.

The thought wouldn't leave her all day and the more she thought, the more she realised just how many times Neil

112

had been late recently. That it might be another woman did not cross her mind, Neil would never do that. But she had smelled drink on his breath once or twice. Perhaps the job was turning him into an alcoholic. She consoled herself with a large slice of chocolate gâteau from the freezer, hardly allowing time for it to thaw properly. There was only one solution. She must ensure he had large, nutritious meals to keep his strength up, and she would make a real effort at bedtime. It would take his mind off things.

Marg would only have laughed if she had known that her husband, at that precise moment, was staring out of his office window wondering if he had the nerve to kill her.

In every town and village throughout England, and probably throughout the world, there is always one family who are well known to the police. Their name is the first one to come to mind when property is broken into or items go missing. Not hard nuts, not big-time villains, but petty thieves who are usually incompetent. They generally get caught and they always do it again and no one can understand why they put themselves to the bother for so little reward.

There were several such families in Rickenham Green, one in Little Endesley – who were suspiciously law-abiding at the moment – and, naturally, one in Frampton. They were called the Coopers. 'Mrs' Cooper went to the bingo on Saturday nights and, on the bus coming home, when she saw someone like that nice Dixon girl she would be curious. How could it be that some women had children who grew up good and clever and didn't cause them any worry whereas her three were nothing but trouble? That some of the blame might lie with herself was not an idea which ever occurred to her. She was the put-upon one.

Holly – named after the Audrey Hepburn character in *Breakfast at Tiffany's* – Cooper was born into the Webster family. They had lived in Frampton for several generations. When Holly became pregnant by one of the Cooper twins it was no big deal. These things happened – had happened, in fact, in both families already. The Websters and the Coopers being friends and neighbours, it was expected that their offspring would set up home together. No one in Frampton had much recollection of the wedding, which was hardly surprising as no such ceremony had ever taken place. Holly and Bob continued living together and produced another two children.

The first, a girl, followed in her mother's footsteps and became pregnant, but not until, at the tender age of seventeen, she was already married. It was a great relief to her parents as her school record, both for attendance and academic achievement, was so poor it was almost non-existent. Her general manner was not one to endear her to a potential employer, had she ever wished to find a job. This eldest child went off with her husband to live in Rickenham and settled down to a life of domesticity.

Next came Sam, then Joe, both registered at birth in these diminutive forms of names. Sam spent his apprenticeship to adulthood in various hostels and institutions in which, instead of becoming a reformed citizen, he learnt further skills in his trade of breaking and entering.

Joe had been in trouble, too, but mainly because he was easily led and looked at Sam as some kind of hero figure. Neither of their parents thought what the boys did was so terrible and, since Sam's first misdemeanour at the age of eleven, they had washed their hands of responsibility. Bob Cooper worked on the land and had finally, at a very low price, purchased the house in which they lived. It was clean and comfortable and they ate well. Neither Holly nor Bob could understand what had gone wrong with their children.

Each Saturday, as the bus bounced its way along the lanes, Holly fully expected a visit from the Rickenham constabulary before the night was out. At one time it was the village bobby who had made regular appearances on their doorstep. Those days had gone. Now it was a panda car from Rickenham.

This weekend had passed pleasantly enough. Too pleasantly, Holly realised, when she saw the white vehicle pull up outside. She ran a comb through her long, blonde hair – nothing like Audrey Hepburn's – and went to answer the door.

'Mrs Cooper?' Holly nodded. She did not know these two. 'Are either of your boys in?'

'Joe is. I don't know where Sam's gone. Come in.' There was no point in delaying things. 'What've they done this time?'

Not, PC Snell noticed, what're they *supposed* to have done. 'We're not saying they've done anything, madam, we're just making some inquiries.'

Holly had heard that one a few times. 'I'll get him down.'

She went up to his room where he lay, half asleep on the bed. On hearing his mother's footsteps he had shoved the pornographic magazine he was studying under the pillow. 'Police,' she said.

'Again?' Joe got off the bed and followed her downstairs.

'Just a couple of questions – Joe, isn't it? Can you tell us where you were on Saturday night?'

Joe's face lit up. For a moment he'd thought they were going to ask about Sunday. 'Sure. My mate came around and gave me a lift into town. We had a couple of drinks in the Feathers then we went to the Nite Spot.'

'What time did you leave there?'

'When it closed. Dunno. Two, I suppose.'

'I heard him come in, he's never quiet when he's had a couple of drinks. It was about quarter-past,' Holly informed them.

'Thank you. And your brother? Any idea where he might've been?'

'Nah. He's got his own friends now.' There was a note of regret in Joe's voice.

'When are you expecting him back, Mrs Cooper?'

'Sam?' She laughed. 'When he's hungry.'

'We'll call back later then, if that's all right with you.'

Holly showed them to the door. Officers Snell and Bishop had been briefed. They knew the adult Coopers would put up no resistance as they had been accustomed to their visits for the last ten years.

'Has he done anything, Joe?' Holly asked when she had shown them to the door.

'No idea. He doesn't talk to me much these days.' She ruffled his hair. Joe, the youngest, and by far the smallest, was her favourite. She had a sneaking suspicion that out of the way of Sam's influence he might make something of himself. Joe went back to his room and his pictures of semi-clad women.

Holly stared out of the window, unaware of the bleakness of the scenery. These winter months of dark skies and barren fields had been part of her life since the day she was born. No greater matter was on her mind than what to cook for her men.

Brian Greenham at the Plough turned the dial of the central heating system anti-clockwise. The body heat of the locals combined with that of the men from the site had warmed the place up in no time. There were even more of them tonight and by the way they were grumbling he hoped they wanted to drown their sorrows. Snippets of overheard conversation told him the job was unlikely to finish on time. The police wanted to interview everyone again, this time down at the station.

'Crazy!' The Goat was saying to the Malone brothers. 'Even if only two of us go at a time, it means whole sections'll be held up.' For certain parts of the work the full team was required. 'Thomas is tearing his hair out.'

'You're right, there – isn't he, Tony? Still, from what I hear, Thomas might have to answer a few more questions himself,' Paddy said.

'You mean about this woman? Married, isn't she?'

'I believe so. I can't make it out, but the rumour's going round it's connected with Gerry's death. Can't make any of it out, meself, now. How did anyone find out about her in the first place?'

'A couple of the blokes've heard him ringing her from the office.'

Paddy Malone altered his position on the tattered plastic seat which ran the length of the wall. The Goat, whose presence he was used to, and whose smell he seemed no longer to notice, could still, at times, be a bit too close for comfort.

Paddy smiled and shook his head. 'That's not exactly proving much. He could have been speaking to one of the girls at head office or anyone.'

'No, sir. According to those who're at Rickenham, yer man was definitely making an assignation and he mentioned a husband and the fact he couldn't be late because of his own wife.'

'Not very nice that, Seamus, listening in on other people's telephone conversations.'

'Not very nice chasing married women, Paddy.'

'You're right, there, Seamus. Still, an hour or so in the warmth of the station house with a nice cup of institution tea won't come amiss. Especially as we get paid for it. Now, Seamus, have I told you about this new feed the wife's bought for the racing turkeys?'

Seamus shook his head. He never made any comment when Paddy talked about racing turkeys or kipper hurling because he could not decide whether he was being made fun of. On the other hand, in the part of Ireland where he came from they raced pigs and it didn't do to show your ignorance. He sat back, at a distance more favourable to the Malones' nostrils, and tried to keep an expression of sceptical interest.

Brian Greenham came to clear away the glasses which were mounting on their table and to empty the ashtray. He didn't know how anyone could sit so close to The Goat. The smell seemed to permeate the whole building. 'You lads all right?'

'Yes, soir, another drop if you don't mind.'

Strange, Greenham thought as he ducked under the counter flap to pour three more pints of Guinness, 'I can't even remember what Daniels looked like now.' Still, it wasn't surprising – he might have slept on the premises but he didn't do much of his drinking there. 'Now this lot,' he said to himself as he placed the drinks on the bar. He didn't need to finish the sentence; there was a smile on his face as he rang another £4.95 into the till.

Paul had arranged to meet Nichola after work on Tuesday. It worked out fine. Nicky had some after-school activity which went on until five and by the time she reached his flat she only had to wait about fifteen minutes for him to get back from work. At the moment he was gardening, although that was not an apt description of what the job entailed. He was actually digging over the small gardens in a row of new houses, removing builder's rubble from the claggy soil. Broken bricks, chunks of hard-set cement and lengths of electrician's wire came to the surface as he repeatedly pushed in the fork with the arch in the sole of his wellington boot. It was satisfying in its own way, a good feeling when the ground was cleared and tidy ready for the grass seed which would be sown in a matter of weeks, although, with the weather still raw, it seemed a long way off. He could not understand how his personal life had become such a mess. 'It's Nicky, really,' he had to admit. He leant on his fork as a sudden fit of shuddering overtook his body. He was experiencing all sorts of symptoms lately yet he'd always thought it daft when he heard other people say falling in love took away your appetite and made you shake. Paul had his own reasons for shaking.

'I'll ask her tonight,' he promised himself.

Paul worked on until it was too dark to see. The physical exertion soothed his nerves and wore him out to the extent that he could sleep at night. At last he cleaned off the fork and put it, along with a few other tools, in the boot of his car.

He drove towards his flat – much tidier these days. As he crossed the traffic lights on Saxborough Road he saw a familiar figure walking slowly along the road. He pulled into the side and tooted. 'Nicky!' he shouted as he wound down his window. 'Get in, you must be freezing.'

At first she made no response. It was as if she did not know he was there. Of course, over the noise of the machinery in the compound and the wind whistling high in the branches of the trees, she might not have heard him. She took one last look over her shoulder and walked reluctantly round to the passenger door.

'What time do you have to be in?'

'Eight forty-five bus.'

'I wish you'd let me drive you. It's daft, you hanging around at bus stops when I've got a car.'

'No. It's too risky. If my parents saw me they'd never let me out in the evenings.'

'I can't understand you sometimes. Why don't you tell them? Most girls your age have got boyfriends.' He paused as he watched in the mirror for a gap in the traffic, then pulled out. 'Are you ashamed of me?'

119

'Of course not.' Not ashamed, not really – it was just that she wanted so much better. The story of her parents being strict and old-fashioned had initially been a way of ensuring that the relationship did not become too cloying. A bit of fun round at Debbie's with Paul was all she had wanted. Before Paul there had been two others. And one since, the one that mattered. And now, for only the second time, she was going to Paul's flat. It put the relationship on to a different level. But she had to ask him. The question was, would he believe her lies?

Sam Cooper, having been warned by his mother and brother that the police wanted to see him about something which occurred on Saturday night, had nothing to fear. He hadn't done anything more than get drunk – and not even to the stage where he couldn't remember what he might have done. Nevertheless, he was not like Holly and Joe, who kept up a pretence of co-operating with the police. He was of the modern world: he knew his rights as a citizen and phrases such as police harassment fell from his lips effortlessly. He could, if he chose, refuse to answer any of their questions. For the time being. He was aware that might soon change but they had to get him into court first. He was perfectly safe this time. There was nothing they could do. He was innocent, and if they tried to make out he wasn't, he would write to his MP and the local paper and generally make them out to be the incompetent idiots he believed them to be.

He did not know that this particular burglary had the 'Cooper' stamp all over it, but that was irrelevant. He did not do it.

'They must've realised they were wrong,' Sam Cooper commented twenty-four hours after PCs Snell and Bishop had first called round. But Sam was wrong, it was just that more important matters had intervened.

When the knock on the door came, all the curtains were drawn against the darkness and the kitchen was warm and steamy and full of cigarette smoke.

Sam decided he would answer their questions, give them no cause to feel insulted or angry by his responses, then make an official complaint. But he would not let them in.

'I'm very sorry,' Sam said, his sly grin belying his words, 'but I would object. If you had a search warrant, well, that'd be a different matter. Shame you've had a wasted journey. I hope you catch whoever did it.'

PC Snell controlled an urge to call this weasly little character something other than his name. The problem was, they had no fingerprints this time. In the sort of weather they'd been experiencing most people would be wearing gloves as a matter of course.

'To save us time, Mr Cooper,' Snell, seeing how the land lay, was sneeringly polite in return, 'maybe you could tell us who you were with on Saturday?'

'I could, but as I haven't done anything, I don't see why I should. And there's nothing you can do about it. Look, my dinner's ready. Cheerio.'

'Little bastard,' Bishop muttered as they walked hurriedly back to the car. They had not been invited inside the house. He turned the ignition and put the heater on full blast. The engine was still warm.

'Don't worry about him. We know who he hangs around with, we'll ask his mates.' Snell shook his head. 'His attitude's different this time. I don't think he did it – that's why he can afford to be more of a pain in the arse than usual. Come on, we'll go and see his nice friends.'

It took another two hours before they discovered where Sam had spent Saturday night. They were so restricted in so many directions these days that it seemed virtually impossible to get at the truth. What made it worse was that it was rarely the innocent who made complaints but the Coopers of this world.

Chas Thomas, also known to many of the officers, put Sam Cooper in the clear. If he was telling the truth. It could easily be checked. Chas talked only because he lived in fear of Sam and felt he was doing him a service by providing an alibi. They had been to a party, held in a barn where the music was mind-blowing, the alcohol plentiful and, although Chas didn't say so, drugs were available. Over a hundred people had attended, a lot of whom knew Sam.

They had had a lift both there and back. Again, Chas decided it might not be a wise move to mention that their driver had also attended the party and was therefore not likely to be in a fit state to drive. Because he was becoming a little tired of being lumped in with the Coopers, Chas made no objection to the two PCs taking a look round his bedsit. Daft thing to ask, he thought as he watched them poke about. From the doorway it was obvious he had nothing to hide for there was nowhere to hide anything.

The room contained a single bed, quite neatly made, a table and two chairs, a sink and a Calor gas burner, and a fourteen-inch television set balanced precariously on a rickety card table. There were no cupboards. Chas's clothes were on hangers hooked up on the picture rail.

'You don't drive, do you?'

'You know I don't.'

'What's this, then?'

PC Snell leant over and examined a rusty tyre jack leaning against the wall.

'I found it.'

'What d'you want it for?'

'I was going to clean it up, see, and sell it.'

'Sell it? How much do you think you'd get for that?'

'Dunno, a couple of quid, maybe.' It was doubtful Chas would have got round to doing any such thing. His intentions rarely became reality. 'Wasn't worth handing it in.'

'No.' PC Bishop sighed. And if it was, he thought, it's even less likely he'd've done so. As he turned around to leave, satisfied that everything was in order, the edge of his shoe nudged the jack; it slid sideways and fell to the floor. As aware as the villains were of their rights et cetera, he stooped to pick it up and stand it back in its original position. He did not want Chas Thomas claiming they'd smashed the place up.

'What is it?' Snell asked, seeing the sudden change of expression on his companion's face.

Bishop straightened up. He was holding the jack as if it was a baby, very carefully and with one hand wrapped in a none too clean handkerchief. 'What do you make of this?'

PC Snell stepped closer and looked. Their eyes met. It could be nothing or it might mean a lot.

'Where did you find this, Chas?'

'I can't remember. Somewhere out in the country. Me and my girlfriend found it. Why, what's wrong? It's only a piece of rusty old crap.'

'We'll have to take it with us. Don't worry, you can have it back. Do you want a receipt?'

'Nah. Don't suppose I could've sold it.'

They put the jack carefully on the back seat of the car. 'I thought it was all rust at first. It's newer than it looks.'

'Could be an accident. Some bloke traps his hand or something while he's changing a tyre,' Snell surmised.

'Pretty bad injury if he did. And why leave it lying around for our friend to pick up?'

'Because he was more interested in getting himself stitched up, I'd imagine. Still, can't be too sure.'

They handed in the exhibit and went back to their duties. The jack lay, temporarily forgotten for a while, in amongst other items of lost property.

9

DC Emmanuel struggled on with the now routine task of rounding up the young citizens who made their living from stealing cars. Some of these cars were sold on so that their various parts could be used to complete another half of an illegal vehicle. Sometimes only the contents were stolen.

'Beats me, man,' Winston Emmanuel commented to anyone who would listen, 'why people leave valuables in their cars at all. Look at this, for instance.' The latest victim, a thirty-four-year-old career woman, had parked in the multi-storey, her pay and display ticket timed at eleven nineteen. She had paid for four hours, giving the thieves some indication that she did not intend returning immediately. It was her day off. She was going to get her hair done and do some shopping. On the back seat, in clear view, she left an expensive leather briefcase, in itself worth a couple of hundred pounds, let alone the inconvenience of losing the paperwork inside it. Beside it lay a pair of binoculars which had been there since an afternoon's racing at Newmarket some time previously. Now both were gone, unlikely to be recovered, and the cost of the broken side window in her executive-type car would add another couple of hundred on to the insurance claim.

So far, Winston reckoned, they had been lucky in that they still had few cases where the thief had lost control and injured someone.

For want of something better to do, but more honestly, in the expectation of a telephone call from Amarilla, he had stayed on later than was his norm. He was a steady and diligent worker but not renowned for putting in extra hours unless a suitable financial reward was at the end of it.

DC Alan Campbell had come to like Winston and had overcome his secret prejudice against anyone who was not Scottish. Head down over his much-loved computer, he replied, 'Mm?'

'I was saying . . . oh, forget it. Why don't we go to the Feathers? You can get plastered on that urine-coloured liquid that passes for alcohol in your part of the world and I'll sip a real drink.'

'Rum?'

There was a look of disdain on Winston's face as he said, 'Don't you know the difference between Africa and the West Indies? I mean a decent pint of beer. Anyway, I'm as British as you are.' Campbell did not agree. He was Scottish.

'All right.' He turned back to the computer to switch it off. 'Just a minute. That lad we were talking about, the one who's held his hand up to eleven offences, there's one here that wasn't reported.'

'Let's see.' DC Emmanuel leaned over his shoulder. 'You're right. Probably didn't think it was worth it.'

'The kid says he ripped out the radio and forced open the door in order to do so. That's got to be worth reporting. The insurance aren't likely to pay out otherwise.'

'The kid's probably mistaken. Cocky little bastard, isn't he?' The boy in question seemed to enjoy his occupation. He kept a note of all the makes and models, going for a different one every time.

'Do you think it's worth looking into?'

'Yeah. We'd better. Might be the car owner has something he'd rather we didn't know about. Tomorrow'll do.'

'How's the rest of it going?' Campbell asked as they made their way out of the building into the cold night air and turned their collars up over their bare necks.

'Not too badly. We're gradually getting round all the car-parks and places of entertainment. A couple of publicans have agreed to fix up those lights which come on automatically once the beam is broken. Should make it safer for people as well as cars. God, it's cold.'

'This is nothing. In the Highlands –'

'Spare me another of your doom and gloom stories, please.'

PCs Snell and Bishop, having handed in the bloodstained jack, thought no more about it as they continued on their patrol.

'It's so bloody boring,' Bishop moaned. No one was all that keen on the country run, driving through the quiet villages where they hardly passed a soul, especially when it got dark so early. Everyone was watching television behind their drawn curtains; the only light came from spasmodic street lamps and the occasional flood of yellowish white which spilt on to the pavement from the neon strips of a village shop.

'It's not for much longer. I don't know why it bothers you, it's an easy number, this. Has anyone done the Dog and Duck?'

Bishop switched on the interior light and glanced at a list. 'No.'

'There you are then. Ten minutes in the warm and maybe a cup of coffee. Can't be bad.'

They pulled into the car-park round the back. It was in almost total darkness and the kitchen area was unlit. One other car was a vague blur in the far corner. 'I can see what they mean,' Snell said. 'Can't see anything round here.'

Wood smoke was in the air. It filled their nostrils and they sniffed appreciatively. The warmth from the stove that burned the logs hit them as soon as they opened the door. No one was inside but the landlord.

'You timed that well,' he said. 'Just this minute opened.' He was polishing steaming glasses straight from the electric washer. 'Didn't get round to this at lunchtime.' He did not appear to be in the least wary at the sight of two uniformed coppers. He had no reason to be. The landlord ran a tight ship. He closed on time and did not go over the allotted twenty minutes' drinking-up. No 'fences' frequented the place; the clientele came mostly from the village itself and could afford the extra pennies he charged above the prices of the Bull. He was a wise man. He knew that certain publicans thought their idiosyncratic hours went unobserved. They were wrong. He'd seen it before. When their licence came up for renewal it might not be granted. True, if there was no trouble and the late serving was not too blatant, a blind eye might sometimes be turned. But he wouldn't risk it. By eleven twenty the bar was empty.

'Can I get you a drink? Soft one, of course. Or a coffee? I don't envy you tonight. I just went out for some logs. It's taken all day to get this place warm.'

Brandy or rum would be more like it but coffee would have to suffice. The filter machine behind the counter was topped up and popping and hissing where water had spilled on to the stand. The landlord poured two cups. 'It's mostly for me in the evenings. I don't take a drink until ten. I've seen what can happen in this trade. Now, I don't suppose you came here for a social visit. What can I do for you?'

'Well, we're running a campaign at the moment, trying to stamp out car thefts. As a part of this we're talking to all the publicans in the area and –'

'Ah, yes. I saw a bit about that in the *Herald* the other week.'

'Yes. I know this is hardly a high crime area, but these things have a habit of spreading. For instance, have you thought about getting some lighting for your car-park?'

'Never been any need, really. Most of my customers are middle-aged and over, and well-heeled. They don't tend to go in for nicking from their neighbours' cars.'

'No, but if they're well-heeled, they're likely to have nice cars and nice possessions. It'd only take one yobbo to find out there were good pickings to be had, especially if you've got no lighting. And think of the safety of your customers. That sort, well, if one of them was to get mugged as they left, I don't suppose it'd do the trade much good.'

The landlord rested his chin in his hand as he leaned over the bar. 'You're right there. I'll see what I can do. Mind you, the council seem to have restrictions on everything around here. I'll have to get something that doesn't require planning permission. Hang on, now you come to mention it, one of my customers did have a window smashed or something the other week. Can't have been serious though, he said it wasn't worth reporting. More than likely it was some kid throwing stones.'

PC Snell had been doing all the talking up to that point. Bishop now added his bit. 'Don't suppose you remember who it was, do you?' For some reason the car jack sprang to mind. Chas Thomas said they'd found it out in the country. Was it possible that Chas was responsible for breaking into a car and stealing it? Frampton was, after all, rural.

'Yes. Man by the name of Thomas. I hardly know him. He's only started using the place recently. Fancies my barmaid, if you ask me. Still, I don't care why they come as long as they keep coming.'

'Heavy drinker, is he? Thomas?'

'No, only the odd pint or two. Why? Oh, I see. You think he may not've reported it because he'd had too much and was going to drive home. No, the old plastic bag wouldn't have worried him.'

'Thank you, sir. Now don't forget about that lighting, will you?'

Snell and Bishop made a note. It was probably nothing, but DC Campbell was mad keen on statistics. This would be another little one he could feed into his computer. Besides, it had given them a reason to hang around in the warm for a few more minutes. If anyone spotted the length of time their car was outside, they had justification.

The first customer of the evening pushed open the door just as they were leaving. He wore a look of mild surprise as he took in the uniforms but, to his disappointment, the landlord told him the reason for their visit. No breath of scandal ever seemed to seep through the hallowed portals of the Dog and Duck.

Paul had been amazed at Nicky's anger. It was the first row they'd had. Not even a row really, just Nicky doing all the shouting. He'd told her he would do anything for her – had already done so, although she didn't know this – but what she was asking was impossible.

'Don't you understand?' he said, trying to reason with her. 'Haven't you any idea how much I love you? I want to be with you all the time, to look after you. I . . . I want to marry you.'

'Marry me?' She had laughed then. 'You couldn't, even if I wanted to. I'm not old enough.'

'What?' Paul clutched at the back of a chair. The whole thing had upset her, she didn't know what she was talking about. The shaking started again. He clamped his teeth in order to try to stop it.

'I'm fifteen, Paul.'

'You're not. Why are you doing this to me?'

'It's true. Ask Debbie. Now you see why you have to help me.'

'Never. I won't do what you ask.'

'I think you will, Paul. Don't you realise what could happen to you? Under-age sex?'

'You'd do that to me, after all I've done for you?'

'What've you done? A few vodkas.'

'No.' He sank into the chair. He would lose her if he didn't do as she requested. Deep down he suspected he would lose her either way. But what hurt most was the sudden, overwhelming realisation that the child she was carrying might not be his.

'What is it, Nicky?' Marie asked her daughter as soon as she walked through the door. 'You look ever so pale.'

'Nothing. I'm just tired.'

'You work too hard. I've never known anyone put so much time into their studies.'

'You know why that is. I don't want to end up like you. Tied to the house. God, it must be so boring.'

'Nichola!' Marie had a desire to slap this beautiful child of hers. It only lasted a split second. She must be patient. In a year or so she would have outgrown this attitude.

'I want to do things, to go to places, I . . .' But she could not continue. Burning tears ran down her face. She ran from the room and locked her bedroom door behind her.

Phil Dixon, unaware of the personal dramas being enacted back in Frampton, drove his lorry carefully and steadily along the autobahn. This trip was timed perfectly. He would be home for his seventeenth wedding anniversary. Marie probably thought he wouldn't remember. As he drove, he was trying to decide what would please her most. An expensive meal at the Country Club or a piece of jewellery? He wasn't in a position to afford both. One day, maybe, when the girls had left home, he might be able to do so.

Phil Dixon, devoted husband and father, had no idea his whole world would collapse before that date.

'Moira!'

'What is it? There's no need to wake the whole neighbourhood.'

Moira came downstairs belting her towelling robe around her. Her blonde shoulder-length hair, as yet unbrushed, was ruffled. It made her look even younger.

'There's no hot water.'

'There must be.'

'There isn't, I tell you. I'm not a fool. Here, see for yourself.' Ian ran the hot tap over the sink full blast.

'Damn. I'll have to get someone in. Don't flap, Ian, it's not cold enough for the pipes to have frozen. Besides, we'd have no water then. I expect the thermostat's gone. I'll boil you a kettle to shave.' Domestic matters such as this were very much Moira's department. She doubted whether Ian could even find the stopcock.

He often shaved downstairs, leaving the bathroom free for Moira who had more regular hours to keep than himself. It was a habit he had developed in the days when he was on shift work, when he tried to get ready quietly so as not to disturb her.

Moira poured the full kettle of boiling water into the washing-up bowl. 'There. Want some toast?'

'Please. Just one slice.'

Now Mark was an adult she no longer insisted on a proper breakfast. Mostly they fended for themselves. Toast or cereal was usually the limit. As she waited for a second kettleful of water to boil, she thought to herself that Ian could just as easily have arranged for a plumber from his own place of work, but his memory where domestic matters were concerned was as reliable as his knowledge as to where he'd left his car keys. Anyway, she was home during the afternoons, it was simpler for her to give a convenient time. More expense. Still, it wasn't like the early days when every penny had to be watched.

Ian took the rectangular mirror from the top of the fridge-freezer and propped it behind the mixer taps over the sink. Daylight was still an hour away. The fluorescent light overhead hummed and unkindly showed up the lines in Ian's face and the deepening crease in his forehead as he contorted his facial muscles to accommodate the blade. The electric razor Moira had once mistakenly bought him lay unused in the drawer of his bedside cabinet. He claimed he didn't feel clean unless he had a wet shave.

He heard Mark's alarm go off, followed by muffled noises from above. 'You're not an art student yet,' Ian told him when his son shambled bleary-eyed into the kitchen, shirt outside his school trousers, cuffs unbuttoned and his hair, which he'd taken to wearing longer lately, flopping into his face.

Mark made no response to this comment, nor to his mother's greeting. His parents had long since given up reprimanding him on what seemed to be lack of manners. This was, and always had been, Mark's way of beginning the day. From a very early age he seemed unable to communicate until at least 10 a.m. No wonder art's his best subject, Moira thought, as she handed him a mug of coffee. All the classes were in the afternoon.

Ian had volunteered to drop Moira off. He didn't like to think of her waiting at the bus stop in the cold and dark. They passed the compound, a constant reminder to Ian of work, before turning off to where Moira's office lay. The men inside the compound were oblivious to the passing traffic and the car which held the policeman investigating the murder of one of their own kind. They had already been at work for an hour and a half. Most of them were settling down again. It was a week and a half since Gerry Daniels died. And no one else had come to any harm.

Moira got out of the car and waved as she hurried towards the door and warmth.

'Good night?' Ian asked as Barry Swan strolled through the door at nine twenty.

'Do I detect a touch of sarcasm? I'm not late, I've been downstairs. Haven't had a chance to take my coat off yet. Anything new?'

Ian was staring at his in-tray, a thing he did more often than at its actual contents. All urgent or important items were placed on his blotter for special attention, or personally delivered by one of the secretaries. This morning the blotter contained nothing more than his idle doodlings.

'Sir?'

'What is it?' DS Emmanuel stood in the doorway, a half-grin splitting his dark face.

'I'm not certain. Two things. They may or may not be connected . . .'

'Will you try and speak plain English? What things?'

'Operation Keyring, sir. DC Campbell discovered a car had been broken into, some of the contents taken, but the crime not reported.'

'And?'

'And two PCs, following up the public awareness side, have come up with the man's name. We've checked with the DVLC. We had the make and model, and a publican came up with the name.'

'Yes. So what?'

'The name is Neil Edward Thomas.'

Winston Emmanuel remained standing by the door, an expectant look on his face. It took several seconds for the importance of what he'd been told to sink in.

'*Our* Neil Thomas?'

'The same.'

'Well done. And tell Campbell so. Anyone been to see him yet?'

'No. We thought you'd probably want to go yourself.'

'Thanks.'

'We'd started checking around garages, to see if anyone had repaired such a car recently. Should we stop now?'

'No. Carry on. We might learn something more.'

Winston departed and a few minutes later Barry Swan returned with tea.

Neil Thomas was confused and nervous and sweating despite the outside temperature when he arrived at the Rickenham Green headquarters accompanied by a uniformed officer.

He was made to wait ten minutes before being told the Chief Inspector was now ready to see him. Ian walked into the interview room and shut the door. He had to do this low key. Thomas might be guilty of nothing at all. It was not as if he'd been involved in an accident and failed to report it. It might simply be that he did not want to lose his no-claims bonus.

'Yes,' Thomas said, finding it hard to breathe when he admitted that was, indeed, the make and registration mark of his car.

'Mr Thomas, was there any particular reason for not informing us your car was recently broken into?'

'No.'

'Hm. What about your insurance company – they won't take too kindly to that, will they?'

'I didn't think it was worth making a claim. Nothing was taken.'

'Nothing? Are you sure?'

Thomas averted his eyes. He was sitting on his hands, presumably to stop them shaking. 'Nothing of any value.'

'Your car radio, I believe.'

Thomas was startled. 'How do you know? Have you found it?'

'No. Surely that's worth something? I mean, a nice car like that, and the damage.'

'The radio didn't work too well. We didn't use it very often. I don't know what all the fuss is about. I've had the car repaired.'

'No fuss, Mr Thomas. Just curiosity. Consider it from our point of view. A man who works with you is murdered, then someone breaks into your car and you don't tell us. It might appear you have something to hide, wouldn't you say?'

Thomas nodded. 'Yes. I can see that. But I can assure you it's nothing like that.'

'What is it like?'

Thomas sighed and bit his lip. Now was the time to admit it. If he tried to conceal it and it came out later, there was every chance Marg would find out. It did not strike him as incongruous that his intentions were to leave her and set up home with Marie, that it wouldn't matter if Marg found out as she had to at some point. Neither did he realise that, deep in his subconscious, he knew he would never have the nerve to go through with it.

'It's nothing to do with Gerry's death, Chief Inspector. I can assure you of that.' Ian decided he would be the judge of that statement but let the man continue. 'I was having an affair, a married lady. My wife doesn't know. I went to the Dog and Duck for a quick drink while I waited for her. She said she'd pick me up outside. Sometimes we went in my car, sometimes hers. I was gone about two hours but I left the car in their car-park. You see, the landlord knows me now. If I'd reported it you'd've found out I wasn't in the pub. So would everyone else and my wife, well, my wife .'

'Yes.'

'I put it right round the back, out of sight of the road. When I got back the door had been forced – it was locked, I'm not that careless. The radio was ripped out and some loose change I kept for parking was missing. There was nothing else to take. I checked the boot. I keep a lot of tools in there. Some of them are for work, nothing was missing.'

135

'But surely your wife noticed the damage?'

'Yes. I lied to her.'

'Are you lying to me?'

'No. I promise you I'm not. I just didn't want her to find out. I said I'd done the damage myself, reversing – it looked possible, the door was dented. I took it to be repaired straight away so she didn't notice the radio was missing.'

'Where did you take the car?'

'Where?' It seemed an odd question. 'Frank's Autos, down by the railway station. They'll confirm it there.'

'All right, Mr Thomas, that's it for now.'

'I can go?'

'You can.'

'Will my wife need to know of any of this?'

'It depends on several factors. I can't give you any guarantees.'

Thomas nodded and went back to the compound.

Ian related the contents of this interview to Barry. 'Oh, shit,' he said.

'What?'

'I totally forgot. You reminded me, saying none of his tools were missing. The lab said the jack was missing from Daniels' car.'

'Is that relevant?'

'Only in that they said everything else was in place, spare tyre new, and that a box of tools in the boot was perfectly looked after. It seemed inconsistent, that's all.'

'The spare was new?'

'Yes.'

Ian picked up the receiver and dialled the number of the lab. It was not Brenda who answered and he had to wait whilst someone went to find the information he wanted.

'Well, that is interesting.'

'What is?'

'You're right. No jack. New spare. But he didn't lose the jack, forget to put it back after changing a tyre or something. None of those tyres has been changed for a long time. The mud scrapings from all four match.'

'But what does any of this mean?'

'I don't know, Barry. He might've lent it to someone who, now he's dead, has decided he may as well keep it. Could've been stolen. Unlikely though. Why just take that? Or, and this is what I think, it was used as the murder weapon. Think about it. A heavy metal object. Traces of rust in the head wound. And Daniels' own car was used to transport him back to the compound. It fits, don't you see?'

'Will this help Brian Lord?'

'I doubt it. But it may help us. It may not've been some long-held grudge. If it was, and the murder was intended, the killer would have gone armed. A jack is not exactly your ideal weapon – can't be hidden, for one thing. No, it's more likely that it was an accidental meeting. Daniels has the boot of his car open for some reason and a row breaks out, or whatever. The killer sees his chance and takes it.'

'And then bundles him into the back of his own car and drives him into Rickenham, dumping him down the tunnel with the compound night lights on.'

'You come up with something better then.'

'I can't. I'd better get downstairs. We haven't got through all the second interviews yet. And before you ask, no, no one's changed their story.'

And no one was willing to speak out against Gerry Daniels. It was as if there was some sort of superstition involved: if they talked, worse things might occur. And deep down no one wanted to dispel the myth that had grown up around him. By destroying their hero they might destroy themselves.

The week dragged to a close. The proprietor of Frank's Autos, Frank himself, confirmed that he had repaired a green Vauxhall Cavalier belonging to Neil Thomas, that he had put on a new door panel and lock and replaced the radio. He showed them a copy of the bill. DS Swan whistled through his teeth when he saw the amount.

Friday passed quietly enough. Faxes were received from northern towns where Daniels' two families resided. Because of the lack of progress locally the Chief decided it was worth interviewing them. West Midlands and Merseyside Police came back with zero.

The front page of that week's *Rickenham Herald* carried a picture of the interior of the tunnel and showed several men 'at work'. They had actually posed for the photograph as it was impossible to get behind the tunnel-boring machinery which was in place. Everyone was smiling, including Neil Thomas and the Clerk of Works. They had gone in about 430 yards, just under a quarter of a mile. They were behind target already. When the thing was complete and the two tunnels joined up, the Mayor was to make the walk through it, along with one or two other local dignitaries, but that was a long way in the future.

Beneath the photograph was a witty caption and an article giving facts and figures about which no one was in the least curious. Most readers turned straight to what interested them, whether it was the sports section, where the success or otherwise of every minor football and rugby side in the area was reported, the classified section or the general news. Hardly anyone read the complete piece about Nelson Enterprises and what they hoped to achieve for the town, and as the progress, or lack of it, concerning Gerry Daniels' murder was not mentioned until almost the last paragraph, most people missed it.

Marie Dixon, however, did not. Her interest in the article was aroused solely because Neil was involved in the job. He had told her what had happened and the problems created. She finished reading and turned the page.

It was impossible for her to know that, in a very small way, she was partly responsible for that death.

138

The only thing brighter during the rest of that week was the weather. Gusts of wind started off at the top of the High Street, seemingly coming from Safeway's car-park. They swept litter down the road as far as the cluster of building societies, stopped, as if having second thoughts, then continued on towards Bradley Court where they spun rotary lines in the small back gardens this way and that, much to the delight of the women who had washing out as it was the first dry day for weeks.

Puddles dried up and mud, instead of sticking to shoes in claggy lumps, became powdered dirt. The wind continued, shifting not only litter but the low grey clouds. Bank after bank off them were sent swiftly over the horizon until, at last, a weak sun, hardly brighter than the whitish sky, filtered through. It was still cold but it seemed more believable that spring might arrive this year.

DCI Roper pulled on his sheepskin jacket. It was still stiff and bulky but he liked the smell of it. It would eventually soften up and hamper his movement less, and the white fleece lining would no longer appear so obviously new. It was his Christmas present from Moira, bought with what he called her ill-gotten gains from the builder's yard where she worked. They met one lunchtime to choose it, Moira having insisted the old one had to go.

He said goodnight to the few people who remained in the building, crossed the polished floor of the reception area and went out through the revolving glass door. He was glad of the coat. The sun had disappeared and darkness was descending. He pulled up his collar and felt in his pocket for his car keys. It was not a night for hanging around.

There were plenty of people about. Friday night. The start of the weekend. Not for him, though – he would be back at work in the morning.

The set of lights he was approaching changed colour. This did not deter the driver in front of him who accelerated on amber and took a right turn sharply, tyres squealing; the driver in the oncoming car blasted his horn.

'Bloody idiot,' Ian muttered.

He drove to the end of Belmont Terrace but was unsuccessful in finding a parking space on his side. He had to reverse quite a long way back and park on the opposite side. It was the last slot. Anyone coming home now would not be pleased as they'd have to use the road which ran parallel.

Ian saw the chink of light through the sitting-room curtains. He let himself in. Mark was watching television. 'Where's your mother?'

'I don't know. She wasn't here when I got home.'

Wonderful. The end of a long, tiring week and no wifely welcome. 'What are the eating arrangements?'

Mark shrugged. 'No idea. I'm trying to listen to this, Dad.' 'This' was a half-hour American comedy series which Ian personally couldn't stand, and by the expression on his son's face, he was not finding it particularly amusing either. But Mark hardly ever showed what he was really feeling. Inwardly, he might, metaphorically speaking, be rolling around with laughter.

Moira did not come in until eight. 'Sorry I'm late,' she said. 'I was round at Deirdre's, helping her organise the charity sale. I ended up staying for a drink, and now I've missed the library as well.'

'I thought you'd given up all those good works.'

'I have. I was just giving her a hand. She manages to make me feel guilty if I refuse. Hungry?'

'Yes.'

'Mark?' she called. 'Do you want anything to eat?'

'No, thanks. I'm going out.'

'Tina again?' Ian asked Moira.

140

'No, she's away for the weekend. He's not very happy about it. He's going out with some friends from school.'

Marie Dixon always treated herself to a bottle of wine on Friday and Saturday nights if Phil was away. She cooked a meal for herself and Kate, then had an evening with the television, a long soak in the bath or a good read. Sometimes in the winter months she took up knitting again, but now the girls were older they wanted shop-bought clothes, the same as their friends wore. Nichola usually had a late pass on Fridays, unless her father was home when, reluctantly, she stayed in.

Kate had come straight in from school, hardly five minutes after Marie left the Dog and Duck, or so it seemed. 'Go in by the fire, you're cold.'

Later they had their meal, Marie putting Nicky's on a saucepan of hot water on the cooker for when she came in.

'Hi,' Kate said. Kate, so pink and warm and innocent, was in her dressing-gown after a bath. Nicky felt a twinge of guilt. Kate loved her and looked up to her and would never be as pretty or as clever. And in that moment Nicky envied her as she never had before.

'Here,' Marie said, handing her elder daughter a mug of coffee. Nicky wouldn't touch cocoa – she said it was fattening. 'Your meal's in the kitchen. You must be starving.'

'I had a burger,' she lied.

'This can't go on. You've got to start eating properly. Do you know how thin you're getting?'

'Leave me alone, please, Mum.'

Kate watched as her sister left the room. It hurt her to see her like that. She followed her upstairs and knocked on her bedroom door.

'It's me, Kate. Can I come in?'

141

There was a mumbling from within. Kate took a chance and opened the door. Nicky was sitting on the bed, almost in tears.

'What's the matter?'

'Nothing. You wouldn't understand.'

'Don't be horrid to me, Nicky.'

'Oh, Kate.'

Kate, at thirteen, instinctively did the right thing. She ran over to her sister and put her arms around her. Nicky buried her head in her shoulder and wept as if she would never stop.

'Don't tell Mum, will you?' she said when it was over. 'She'll only start asking questions. I'm all right now. Really.'

Kate smiled and went back downstairs again.

'Is she all right?'

'Yes.' Kate nodded and kept her eyes fixed on the television set. She did not want to have to lie to her mother.

Marie sighed and did likewise, but she was not able to concentrate. How could she hope to understand what was going through the mind of her fifteen-year-old when she couldn't begin to understand herself at the moment? She had everything she'd ever wanted: a husband whom she still loved and fancied like mad, a home and two healthy children. Why on earth had she begun an affair with a man older than herself, one who was not even as attractive as Phil and who took life so very seriously? In fact, she suspected that, on a full-time basis, Neil Thomas was extremely boring.

'It really has to stop,' she told herself, pouring another glass of wine. 'Next time, without fail, I'll tell him.'

Nichola had not met Paul that night. She had to sort something out. He had failed her; there was only one other course to take.

She had watched and waited for a long time, her fingers and toes numb with cold, becoming more miserable with

142

every second that passed. In the end there was nothing else to do but catch the seven forty-five bus home.

'Take the morning to go through these statements,' the Chief told the assembled CID officers. Not all of them were on duty, but there were enough to tackle the task. 'I want each man's initial account compared word for word with the second one. Whatever's wrong, whatever's not quite synchronised, may not be in the words themselves but in the emphasis. This whole thing is impossible. Somebody has to know something. I'll be in my office.'

He sat for almost an hour, not moving, not really even thinking, just trying to clear his mind to leave room for a logical explanation to float into it. He failed.

At eleven he went down the two flights of stairs to the basement canteen. Although it was mid-morning, a natural time for a break, there were only three uniforms and one other person. That other person was WPC Judy Robbins.

At first Ian didn't recognise her, although her dark clothing was not unlike her uniform. 'Judy? What're you doing here?' The funeral was at two thirty that afternoon. Moira was meeting him here as she had the car, and they were going together. 'Let me get you a coffee.'

She nodded and sat slowly down in one of the tubular chairs.

Ian returned with two mugs and placed them on the table. Judy was unnaturally pale and there were dark circles under her eyes. 'I had to come in. I should've come to work, I think. This week's been unbearable. I wanted the funeral sooner. It sounds awful, I know, as if I can't wait to get him out of the way.' Her eyes filled with tears. Ian gave her some screwed-up tissue from his pocket. 'I'm sorry. I just wanted something, well, normal, before this afternoon. I don't know how I'm going to get through it.'

143

'Moira and I will be there. You can come back with us after.'

'Thank you. It's not very normal in here, is it? It's so quiet, it's like a morgue.' The word held no personal connotations for her, not whilst she was in the station. They bandied about such words all the time.

'It is quiet. Everyone's out chasing car thieves or going through the Daniels statements.'

'I read about that. I didn't really take it in.'

'How's everything else?'

'I've started going through Dad's things.' She smiled wanly. 'He's kept some really odd things, you know. I haven't quite made up my mind yet, but I'm beginning to think I may give up my flat and move into the bungalow. It's not in quite such a bad state as I thought. I mean, I'd have no rent to pay, I could afford to have it done up bit by bit. I just, well, I just can't bear the thought of selling it.'

'There's no rush. You need to get this afternoon over first.'

'I know.' And she did. Judy had dealt with the bereaved often enough. She knew the funeral was an important part of grieving; it was a proper goodbye and those who did not attend missed out on something. 'No one'll mind if I stay here, will they?'

'Of course not. Want another cup?'

'I'll get them.'

'No. Not today. When you're back at work I'll expect your usual brand of self-assertiveness. But not until then.'

Ian left after another fifteen minutes. He tried to remember how he had felt when his parents died, quite quickly, within a year of each other. He had wondered if he ever loved them at all. There were few tears and, at first, he hardly thought of them. Only much later did memories come back to him. It wasn't coldness on his part, he was sure of that, but they were in their forties when he was born and the generation gap, especially then, back in the

1940s, had seemed immense. They might almost have been his grandparents.

But there was a difference. At the time of his parents' deaths he was married to Moira and the father of a small boy. Judy had no other relatives, no boyfriend, and her relationship with her father had been closer than anyone's he could think of.

Back in his office he wondered why he'd bothered to come in. Nothing had been achieved; but he had had a chat with his favourite WPC. Barry called in briefly but was rushing off somewhere with Lucy whom he left sitting in the car outside.

'Want me in later?' he asked.

'Can't see the point.'

'Okay. See you.'

'Barry?' Barry paused in the doorway. 'Do you think it's Thomas?'

'He's the only one who crossed my mind, but he isn't cracking if it is.'

'No. Well, go on then, off to your shopping or whatever.'

But somehow a space had been made for other thoughts to filter through. It was all surmise, even the fact that Daniels may have had a woman, any woman. 'But supposing he did,' Ian reckoned. 'We know Thomas has. And that only came out because of the car thing, it wouldn't have otherwise, I'd bet on that. Now surely someone in that compound must've known. Known but not said. And just suppose for one second that Gerry Daniels was seeing that very same woman.' He stood up and in one swift movement was at the door.

'Barry!' he called as he ran down the stairs. But he was too late. 'Damn him.' He paused. His visit was going to be official, therefore he needed to take someone with him.

In the general office the men were seated, heads bent over paperwork or computers. An idea struck him.

'Sir?' DC Alan Campbell had seen him.

145

Ian shook his head. 'It's nothing. Carry on.' He went to find the duty sergeant and, satisfied with the answer to his question, returned to the canteen.

Judy Robbins was chatting to the girl serving behind the counter. Trade was extremely slack.

'Judy.' Ian took her arm and led her to one side. 'Under the circumstances this is going to sound like a strange request, but do you fancy a trip out to Frampton? I've got to interview someone.'

'But I've –'

'Just say no and I'll understand totally.' He saw that she didn't want to refuse, that she was there because she had no idea what else to do with her time, and that she was lonely and desperate to feel part of something, even if it was only work.

'I've checked your rota. You would be on this morning.'

'Yes. I'll get changed.'

'I'll meet you at the car. I'll just let the sergeant know the score. I expect he'll give you the shift.'

There was a faint tinge of colour in WPC Robbins' face as they made their way through the town, out past the Golf and Country Club, and turned into the B road which led to Frampton. Being back in uniform, having something to do other than the painful business of sorting out her father's possessions, gave her the feeling that life might, after all, continue.

'You're not doing this out of pity, are you?'

'Good heavens, girl, you know me better than that.'

She did know him quite well and that was why she asked. He was a kind and fair man but she knew he was lying. It didn't matter. It had dragged her from the depths of self-pity, a trait she disliked in others and despised in herself.

Ian slowed through the village and Judy watched out for the right address. 'Here' she said, 'this one.' Ian pulled on to the grass verge and they got out of the car. It looked as if someone was at home. A car was parked inside the wide, wooden gate, on the gravel that surrounded the bungalow and obviously saved a lot of gardening. Smoke curled from the chimney, the spiral bending and breaking in half in an air current.

The best that could be said for the property was that it was nondescript. Neither ugly nor over-ornate, neither dilapidated nor spruce. The pebble-dash exterior was a pinkish grey, the paintwork had lost its gloss but was not peeling and the curtains were backed in some cream material, their colour not apparent from the outside.

Ian rang the bell. Its tone was in keeping. No chimes or cutesy melody, a simple, old-fashioned shrill ring which continued as long as his finger depressed it.

The door was opened by a woman whom, at first, Ian thought more likely to be Thomas's mother than his wife. He had chided Swan often enough about his chauvinistic views, insisting that looks were not everything, but in this instance he found it almost understandable that Thomas had broken his marriage vows. The woman in question said her husband was in.

Having produced their identity, although none was asked for, they were shown into the front room. Even Judy, in her state of unhappiness, found it hard not to gasp when Mrs Thomas first stood before them. Her chins were numerous and almost rested on her shoulders; her eyes, when she spoke, disappeared in folds of flesh. As for the rest of her body, it was difficult to see where one part started and another ended. She wore a full, dark purple skirt and a salmon pink Orlon jumper. Her feet were clad in brown, mock leather slip-ons, the flesh around her ankles spilling over the sides. Judy did not believe she had ever before seen anyone so large that they had to turn slightly sideways to get through a normal-sized doorway.

Neil Thomas hardly noticed their entrance. He was reading a newspaper, ignoring the television which was turned to a sports channel. He imagined the caller to be some friend of his wife's, and that they would take themselves to the kitchen to drink tea and gossip.

'Neil?' He looked up. Ian noticed he did not start or gasp or fiddle nervously with the paper. Had he seen them approach and prepared himself or were these the actions of an innocent man?

'I need to ask you a few more questions, Mr Thomas. I'm sorry to trouble you on a Saturday afternoon, but we thought it was easier this way than dragging you into Rickenham.'

'Oh, about the murder?'

'Yes.'

Thomas was making it clear to his wife that there could be no other possible reason for them being there. He was also, with his eyes, pleading with them not to mention Marie Dixon. Had they been to see her, to check on his story, and caused trouble between her and her husband? He would never forgive himself if that was the case. They hadn't, not yet. They wanted to hear what he had to say first.

'May we talk in here?' Thomas nodded. The room was warm, the coal fire belting out a decent heat. The interior was only a little better than the exterior of the property. Everything was clean and tidy but lacked both imagination and plain co-ordination. The furniture was of mixed periods, the carpets and curtains unmatched. The impression Ian got was one of impermanence, as if the occupiers had not bothered to do much with the place since they wouldn't be there long. Such was not the case. Marg Thomas cared only about warmth and food and her husband's well-being. Neil didn't notice his surroundings.

'It's bitter, isn't it? I expect you could do with a cup of coffee?'

'Yes, please.' Ian saw what he was about. He wanted Mrs Thomas out of the room for a while.

'She won't know, will she?'

148

'No.'

'And Mrs Dixon?'

Ian did not answer. 'Mr Thomas, I'll ask you quickly, whilst your wife's not in the room, was Gerry Daniels having an affair with Marie Dixon also?'

'No. Definitely not.'

'How can you be so sure?'

'Take my word for it, I am.'

'Has anyone suggested to you it might be so?'

Thomas's hesitation was minimal but it was enough. 'No.' That hesitation ensured Marie Dixon was going to get a visit.

'All right. About your car –'

'I've explained about that. My wife –'

'Oh, the car.' Marg entered the room awkwardly, a tray in her hands. On it were four matching mugs advertising a brand of coffee granules. Steam rose from them. There was no milk jug, only a sugar bowl. Black coffee, which Ian would have preferred, was out of the question. 'It's unlike Neil, you know – Inspector, is it? He's such a careful driver. Well, he's a careful man in most ways. So silly backing into a wall. Still, in the sort of weather we've been having, it's not easy to see when you're reversing. He didn't hit anything, did he? Neil, you didn't hit another car, did you?' She looked from one man to the other.

'Nothing like that, Mrs Thomas.' He and Judy accepted their mugs of coffee. It looked almost like hot milk and when Ian sipped it he realised it had been made with boiled milk, full cream. He wouldn't be able to finish it.

'Mr Thomas, when did you last change a tyre?'

'On my car? I've no idea. Not for years, I don't think. I had two new ones with the last MOT.'

'That's your car outside, isn't it?' He knew it was. It was the same model and registration number they had made inquiries about with Frank's Autos.

'Yes.'

'Would you mind getting your keys? We'd like to take a look in the boot.'

Thomas was too puzzled to question their reasons. Obediently he placed his mug on the tray and went to get the keys. Outside he stood shivering while Ian undid the boot and lifted the lid. No words were exchanged as he went over the whole vehicle; the boot, the interior and the engine. Everything was just where it should be. Spare tyre legal, appropriate tools for changing it in place. It was much like the bungalow, neat and clean, no sweet wrappers on the floor and the ashtray empty. Ian bet it was probably taken to the car-wash at regular intervals.

'I'd like you to have a good think, Mr Thomas. About anything pertaining to Gerry Daniels. You see, I believe he did know Marie Dixon.'

'No.'

'Pardon?'

'No. He was just taunting me.' At last. An admission.

'How do you mean?'

'I was careless, some of the men overheard me speaking to her on the office telephone. That's the only way he could've heard her name.'

'Really? I would've thought you'd only use her first name in a telephone conversation.'

'I do. Of course I do. They found out where she works, and they checked. They don't like me, you know. They resent my position of authority.'

'And you believe someone deliberately went out of their way to find out her surname, just so as they could taunt you?'

'Yes. You don't know what it's like there.'

Ian had just realised the time. 'All right, Mr Thomas, we'll leave it like that for now. We'll be in touch again.' He and Judy went back to the car.

'At least we didn't have to drink that disgusting coffee,' she commented as they set off. 'Are we going to see Marie Dixon now?'

'No, Judy, time's getting on.'

'Oh. Yes.' Ian saw her profile droop. But it wasn't so bad. If she had forgotten the time, her mind, at least temporarily, had been taken off what lay ahead that afternoon.

'I want this woman interviewed,' the Chief said. 'Any of you that's free this afternoon. Find her address. It's got to be Frampton way somewhere – Thomas sometimes met her outside the Dog and Duck. Tread carefully. From what we've got, it could be no more than an affair. Don't go breaking up a marriage if you can avoid it.' That was his reason for being so easy on Thomas, that and the fact that he had to make sure Judy was back in time to change.

'Why didn't I get someone round to see her before?' he asked himself. It seemed an obvious thing to do. Now, it did. But not then. Not when there had seemed to be no connection between the dead man and a woman Thomas was seeing on the side.

Moira arrived in plenty of time and they made their way to the cemetery grounds, inside which was a small chapel. Judy refused the offer of a lift; she was going with Lucy who was her best friend and whom she'd known for years. Lucy was picking her up at her flat, guessing that, whatever Judy thought, when the time came she would not be up to driving a car.

Ian was very pleased to see how many people attended. Judy sat in the front of one of the rows of seats which ran lengthways down the chapel. There were no other relatives. She was flanked by Lucy and Barry Swan. One or two others from the station had turned up, out of respect to Judy, not because they had necessarily known her father.

There were candles on the altar, and the coffin, when the pall-bearers placed it on the trestles in the middle of the rows of seats, was gay with flowers and wreaths. The service was tasteful and appropriate and unspoiled by unnecessary eulogistic phrases. Fred Robbins had been a kind, decent man, living by his own personal code of behaviour. He liked a drink and he enjoyed a game of darts. He had left no mark on the world unless it was in the shape of his daughter. His burial was as dignified as his life had been, and even the funereal weather gave way to a winter sun.

'It's over,' Judy said, tears running down her face. 'And my God, I'm going to miss him. Right . . .' There was a touch of the old Judy as she pulled back her shoulders. 'I haven't organised anything official, but I thought that as the bar of the Queen's Hotel is open all afternoon, we might go there. I rang this morning and they said they could arrange a few plates of sandwiches.' She looked around hopefully. Most of those present agreed to go.

While the funeral was taking place DC Campbell, having found Marie Dixon's address, drove over to Frampton to interview her. The outcome was disappointing.

Marie was willing to answer all his questions, and did so quite honestly, more relieved than Campbell could know that her husband was away and both her girls out. Yes, she had been having an affair; no, she had never met Gerry Daniels. The only reason she knew his name was because Neil had mentioned it and she had read about his death in the *Herald*. Campbell believed her.

At the end of the week, it occurred to PC Diamond, who was sorting lost property, that something ought to be done about that jack which was lying around. Had Ian or anyone in CID been aware that it was in the building, and had been for some time, all hell would have broken loose. They were looking for such a thing – possibly. There was no real evidence to prove that the missing jack was the murder weapon, and there were many other reasons why it might not have been in the boot. Always supposing Gerry Daniels had owned one in the first place.

However, PCs Snell and Bishop had not forgotten it, although they were unaware that no one in CID knew of its existence – communication between the two branches was still far from what it should be. They assumed that someone had done something about it, which only proved that even within the uniformed branch communication was far from perfect. They did, however, question Chas Thomas's girlfriend, Suzanne, who confirmed that they had gone for a drive in her car, then a walk.

'In this weather?' Snell asked.

'Why not? Besides, Chas wanted a fag and I don't let anyone smoke in my car. We weren't out long, a few minutes. Chas tripped over it, it was lying in the grass by the side of the road.'

'Whereabouts?'

'I couldn't say exactly. Somewhere along that narrow road just before you come into Frampton.' Suzanne shrugged. She couldn't see what all the fuss was about. As far as she was concerned it was a rusty piece of old junk. She knew nothing about changing tyres or putting oil in, her dad saw to all that for her.

'We haven't got anyone in hospital, have we? No serious assaults outstanding?' PC Bishop said when the interview was over.

'Nope. Mind you, we've got a murder.'

'Oh, shit. We've been thinking it might be useful in Operation Keyring, we never gave that a thought.'

Both men were very quiet. They knew how Daniels had died. But a jack? They were tense, bracing themselves for what was to come. They should have made more of it at the time. Hopefully, whoever they'd left it with had done the necessary.

Moira had to drive back from the Queen's Hotel. The drink had flowed plentifully and several of the participants had asked the manager if they might leave their cars in his car-park overnight. Judy declined their offer to go back with them and stayed on. Her eyes were bright, her cheeks flushed, and Moira hoped she'd get well and truly drunk and sleep all through Sunday. She looked exhausted.

Ian was at that stage she hated, where the drink made him bad-tempered and belligerent. She'd pour him another one or two when they got home. The next stage after belligerence was carefree and loving. She'd prefer his pawing and amorous suggestions – which didn't lead anywhere – to this non-stop carping.

Later she looked at him fondly as he lay slumped in his armchair, sound asleep in front of the football. She did not make the mistake of turning it off, he always woke immediately. Yet the voice of the raucous commentator disturbed him not one bit.

His hair was untidy, his shirt half out of his trousers and his stomach, in this relaxed position, hid his belt. She kissed him on the forehead and went up to bed with a book.

10

Tom Clancey's conscience was getting the better of him. He returned to the Station Arms at ten thirty on Saturday evening and had another word with Gloria.

Gloria lit a cigarette and blew out a long stream of smoke towards the extractor fan which was rattling inefficiently between the bricks of the outside wall. 'This is the second time you've mentioned this row, Tom. If it's playing on your mind, for goodness sake, go and tell them. All right, you say it mightn't mean anything, and I'm beginning to get a good idea what it's like to work there. You can't go around telling tales on the other men. But have you thought, it might be relevant? You hear a man threaten to kill someone and the next minute he's dead? He might've done it.'

'Not him, he hasn't got the balls.'

'I wouldn't be too sure. You never know what anyone's capable of until they're pushed. Have another drink. On me. And go and see them in the morning. No point now. Saturday night, they'll be up to their eyes in drunks and fights.'

Tom laughed. After some of the cities he'd worked in, Rickenham Green seemed like a haven from the troubles of the real world. But he would do as she suggested. He was beginning to get on his own nerves. For this evening he would do his best to boost her takings.

DCI Roper did not arrive at headquarters until ten thirty. Three aspirins washed down with a glass of cold water, a bacon sandwich smothered in HP sauce and several mugs of black coffee had done nothing to dispel the throbbing of the timpani band apparently performing in the region of his skull. An iced bottle of mineral water – which he normally wouldn't be seen dead drinking – purchased in the canteen along with several more cups of black coffee, did not even begin to slake his thirst. He lit a cigarette with shaking hands and almost gagged.

'The first one's always the worst,' Barry told him. 'Keep at it, they get better.' Ian ignored both the man and his comment just as Mark had earlier ignored *him* when he snapped at him over the breakfast table. He may not have

155

heard though, because he was wearing his headphones at the time, from which a tinny, regular scratching issued. Moira, when he complained that the bacon wasn't crisp enough, snapped back and told him to go to work, although in stronger terms than those.

'Whatever did you do last night to get in this state? You weren't too bad at the Queen's.'

'Blame my dear wife. It wouldn't surprise me if she spiked my drinks.'

'Ah, I see.' Good old Moira, she knew how to handle her husband. 'Better have a hair of the dog at lunchtime.' The look Barry received was venomous.

Ian went to replenish his coffee cup and scrounged a couple more painkillers from Betty, who was on canteen duty. She seemed to carry a first-aid kit in her copious handbag, which made her a great favourite with her customers.

'Now, do you want to hear my news, or not?'

'What news?'

'Lucy and I have decided we might as well get married.'

'Married? You?'

'Well, don't act so surprised, it was on the cards.' Barry was hurt. He was expecting congratulations.

'Sorry. She's a nice girl. You could've done a lot worse.' His engagement almost damned with faint praise, Barry accepted that was the best he could hope for from the Chief this morning.

He had been in his office ten minutes, a second cigarette, as Barry said, tasting better, and was wondering how he could get anything purposeful achieved during the day when his internal phone rang.

'Have him taken to an interview room. I'll be down in a minute,' Ian said. 'At last. Perhaps they'll all start coming out of the woodwork.' A man named Tom Clancey had something to tell him. He was right, people had been hiding something.

'Mr Clancey? How do you do.' Ian shook his hand, an action Tom was not expecting. 'We've met before.'

'Yes.'

'You have something you wish to tell us?'

'I do. It was only something I overheard, and not a whole conversation, so I might be wrong.'

'What exactly did you hear, Mr Clancey?'

Tom pressed his lips together then sighed. 'I don't like doing this. Well, I'm here now. I overheard the agent, Neil Thomas, saying to Gerry that he would kill him if he didn't stop spreading rumours.'

'Gerry? You mean Gerry Daniels?'

'Yes.'

'Is that all?'

'I heard the name Dixon mentioned and, well, we knew Mr Thomas was seeing a married woman with that name.'

'How did you know this?'

'Because a couple of the lads overheard a telephone conversation.' Thomas had said the same thing, but how did they know her surname? He asked.

'I'm not sure. Gerry seemed to know it, though.'

'This lady, she works in a pub out in Frampton. Did anyone make a special journey out there to discover her name?'

'Not as far as I know. Why should they? No one was particularly interested. Gerry just used it to wind Thomas up. Thomas didn't like him, that's a well-known fact, but I really don't think he killed him.'

'Any reason why he didn't like him?'

'Jealousy. Not over the woman, I don't mean, but generally. Thomas doesn't get on with anyone much, but I think he was jealous of people like Gerry. He was a great worker, and fearless, and he liked a good crack.'

'You mean Thomas doesn't like people who live life to the full?'

'Yes, that's exactly it.'

157

The Chief could understand that, having seen his home and his wife. The man seemed to have nothing worth living for. And he had tendencies towards paranoia. Why else would he have convinced himself someone had made an effort to find out exactly who Marie was?

'Is there anything else, Mr Clancey?'

'No. I just felt I had to tell you.'

'Why now and not when we first spoke?'

Tom's cheekbones reddened. 'It's not done. And I thought you'd find out all you needed to know anyway.'

'It's not that simple, you know. We nearly always need the public's assistance to solve cases.'

'I'm sorry.'

'Forget it. Thanks for coming in.'

Tom Clancey left, feeling relieved he had said his piece. It might make no difference but he felt better.

'It still doesn't make sense,' Barry said when Ian told him of the latest development. 'Marie Dixon claims never to have set eyes on Daniels, so how come a. he knew her name, and b. used it to taunt Thomas?'

'Perhaps Dixon's lying. Her husband's away a lot. She's having one affair, why not two? And she fits the theory. Married lady, provides him with a meal, et cetera.'

'And has two teenage daughters. Where are they whilst she's exercising her culinary skills? Unless her husband's very broad-minded she's hardly likely to invite a lover home knowing one of the girls would probably mention it.'

'The husband. You've got something there, Swan, old boy. Maybe that's exactly what did happen. One of the daughters told him Mummy had been entertaining a nice man in his absence and he bumps him off.'

'We'd better go and see her ourselves, hadn't we?'

The sun, now high in a bright blue sky, made a mockery of the weeks of below-zero temperatures. It was as if winter had never been. It was not warm enough to do without a coat but people seemed to smile more readily.

'How's the hangover?' Barry asked as they strapped themselves into the car.

'Lingering, that's why you're driving.'

Marie was hanging out washing when detectives Roper and Swan rang her front door bell. She only heard it when they rang for a second time and came round the side of the house, which was quicker than going through it, drying her hands on her apron.

'Again?' she inquired when Ian told them who they were. 'Someone was here yesterday. Look, we'd better go in. It's colder than it looks out here.'

Marie Dixon obviously wasn't afraid of housework. In the kitchen, into which she'd shown them, every surface gleamed and shone and there were a couple of damp patches where the floor had been washed but had not quite dried.

'Would you like some coffee or do you get sick of being asked that?'

'I wouldn't mind. Thank you,' Ian said. 'Black for me.'

She filled the kettle and busied herself with mugs and the coffee jar.

'I told the man yesterday – Mr Campbell, was it? – that I'd never met this Gerry Daniels. Didn't he believe me?'

'It's not that he didn't believe you, Mrs Dixon, but we're just making further inquiries.'

'Ah. I see.' She had watched enough crime drama on the television to recognise the neat way of saying they did think she was lying.

'There's something puzzling us. Why do you think Mr Daniels used your name to taunt Mr Thomas? We are, by the way, fully aware of the relationship between the two of you.' Marie did not blush but she did bite her lower lip nervously.

'I really couldn't say. I don't know how he knew my name, or anything about me. I'm absolutely certain Neil wouldn't have said anything. Please don't think I'm

159

naïve – I know men have a tendency to boast about such things, especially when there's a lot of them working together – but Neil isn't like that and he's terrified his wife might find out. Actually, it's over, the relationship as you call it.'

'Over?' This was news. Thomas hadn't said so.

'As far as I'm concerned. You can't imagine how bad I feel about it. I meant to end it this week, but...' She shrugged, still unable to explain to herself why she had not done so. 'I'm sorry. You didn't come here to listen to my personal problems.'

'Does your husband know?'

'Phil? Good God, no. I don't know what I'd do if he ever found out.'

'More to the point, Mrs Dixon, what would *he* do?'

She stared at him helplessly. 'I really don't know.'

'Is he a violent man, your husband?'

'Not at all. He's never laid a hand on me or the girls. What are you implying? You don't think Phil killed this man? You do, don't you? You believe I did know him and that Phil found out and killed him.' Ian had to admire her rapid, and correct, deduction. 'That's ridiculous.'

'Where's your husband now?'

'In Germany and heading east. He's a lorry driver.'

'How long is he usually away?'

'It varies. He tries to get several jobs. You know, a load from England to somewhere in Europe, then a second one, say, from France to Italy, then another load to come back with.'

'Do you keep a note of his trips?'

'Not as such but I mark them on the calendar. Here.' She unhooked it from the wall above a plastic-coated ring through which a tea towel was folded.

Ian took it, glanced at it and raised his eyebrows. 'Oh, the dates circled are when he's coming home, the ones crossed through when he's going again.' If Marie's marks were accurate, Phillip Dixon had been in Rickenham on the night of the murder. They would have to check with his employer to be certain and then there was the rigmarole of getting in touch with the various foreign agencies to get him home for questioning or having them hold him until they could get a man out there. They would need the registration mark of his vehicle.

'He's self-employed,' Marie told them. 'Does he need to be involved? Oh, Kate. Come in and shut the door. My younger daughter, Kate.'

'Hello,' 'Hi,' the one from Ian, the other from Barry. Kate stood shyly in the doorway. It did not appear as if she was used to seeing strange men seated at the kitchen table.

'These are policemen,' Marie explained. 'They've just come to ask a few questions. I can give you a contact number,' she continued, turning back to Ian. 'The man's name is Cyril George. He sorts out Phil's jobs and routes and things.'

'Mum, has something happened to Dad?' Kate's face was ashen. The three adults realised how it might look to her.

'No, darling, nothing at all. It's just to do with something at work.' She looked back at her two visitors, her face defying them to say anything otherwise. They both speculated as to whether she had become an adept lier.

There was little more they could do for the moment. If Marie Dixon maintained she did not know Daniels, they could not force her to say otherwise. They left then. The next move was to check on Phillip Dixon's whereabouts on that fatal night.

Ian, his headache now no more than a gentle reminder of yesterday's self-abuse, and in the knowledge that they had at last got a lead, however tenuous, regained his usual good humour.

'What's all this wedding nonsense then? I never thought I'd live to see the day, I must admit.'

'I'm getting on a bit now, and Lucy's twenty-eight. We didn't want to leave it too late if we're going to have kids.' Barry with children seemed an inconceivable idea. 'We're not doing the full bit. Registry office and a few friends. And Lucy's parents and her brother, of course.'

'Get on with them, do you, the future in-laws?'

'I do, actually. Lovely place they've got. Near Market Harborough. They're quite sort of county but very gentle types. Never in a rush and nothing's too much trouble.'

'Easy to be like that when you're loaded.'

'Cynic.'

'Your parents?'

'They don't even know yet. I'll give them a ring tonight, if I can remember the time difference. I don't suppose they'll bother to come back for it, not unless they've got leave due. You and Moira'll be invited, of course.'

'I should hope so. I can't wait to see the day the infamous Swan gets hitched. I don't suppose we'll be able to get hold of this Cyril George bloke today. This is a business card she's given us.'

'Probably lives in the same town – we could find his home address. There's one thing I've just thought of.'

'What's that?'

'If Dixon *is* our man and he finds out we're on to him, he may decide not to bother to come back.'

'Then we shall have to rely on our European counter-parts. We're all one big, happy family now.'

They pulled into the station car-park. Ian was genuinely pleased for Barry, Lucy was a fine girl, but he also experienced that twinge of relief married men get when another of their sex is safely netted. He had envied Barry's freedom, the endless succession of women, but only theoretically. Had he been offered the choice of the world's most beautiful concubines he would have refused. He could not be unfaithful to Moira.

162

'More fuel is required, I think,' Ian commented when they were back at the station. 'A nice spot of Betty's liver and onions'd go down a treat. Want to join me?'

'Just for coffee. I'm taking Lucy out tonight, to celebrate. Won't Moira be cooking for you later?'

'I doubt it,' Ian said enigmatically, remembering his comments about the bacon sandwich. 'Ah, Markham. Have you heard the news?'

DS Markham mooched in through the swing doors, hands in pockets, deep in thought.

'Sir?'

'Swan here has got himself engaged.'

'Has he? That's nice.' And with that he approached the counter and stared hard at the overcooked food disintegrating further under the heat lamps.

Barry shrugged and flicked a saccharin tablet into his coffee. At least Markham had acknowledged the fact, which was more than he was expecting.

'Thomas . . .' Barry said thoughtfully. 'If he has the power to sack men on the spot and he really hated Daniels that much and/or believed he was knocking off his own piece on the side, why didn't he do that? Sack him?'

'I think Thomas is afraid of his own shadow. He may have lost his temper and threatened him but surely he has to answer to somebody if he fires a man. Apart from which, don't forget how popular Daniels was. If he went others might follow or refuse to work.'

'Yes, but there must be thousands out there looking for a job.'

'It's time. You've heard how they work on these projects, everything's worked out to the day and every day over the time means money lost. Fines and penalty clauses.

'Right. That wasn't bad. Back to work. I'll give Cyril George a try. If not, we'll leave it until tomorrow. Dixon presumably has no idea we're interested in him, a few more hours can't hurt.'

Before he even picked up the telephone, DS Markham interrupted him. 'There's something you ought to know about, sir. I don't think you're going to be very happy.' Ian waited. 'One of the local yobbos was in possession of a jack. Bloodstained. Claims he found it out near Frampton and there seems no reason to disbelieve him. His girl-friend alibis him.'

'Great.' Why should he be unhappy to hear this news?

'It was handed in a few days ago. Uniform branch. And nothing's been done with it.'

'What? Who's responsible?'

'A couple of PCs.'

'I want their names and I want to speak to their ser-geant.'

'Yes, sir. I've looked at the jack. It's definitely blood and it's newer than it at first appears. I've had it sent, express, to the lab and arranged for someone to be there to receive it.'

'Well done, Markham.'

'They thought it might be of interest to DC Emmanuel, sir. Operation Keyring. They didn't connect it with the murder. I don't suppose they were aware –'

'It's all right, you needn't make excuses for them. They will have to be spoken to.'

But not now, Ian thought, not until he was no longer angry.

He was almost certain the blood on the jack would turn out to be that of Gerry Daniels and that it was, indeed, the murder weapon. Fingerprints would be ideal but how many people had handled it after the murderer? Chas Thomas, who found it, possibly his girlfriend, PC Bishop, and God knows how many other officers. And it had been chucked into the grass, at that time wet with melted snow and rain. There was very little chance of coming up with enough to make an identification.

DS Swan had already gone home. At four Ian decided he might as well go too. There was no reply from Cyril George's number, only a recorded message on the answering machine. Ian gave instructions for his home address to be traced and for someone to speak to him the minute he was found. At the same time he carefully worded a message to be faxed to all the ports that Marie Dixon had said her husband travelled through. He had a passport and documentation, he had to show them somewhere. Whatever happened tonight, Cyril George would presumably be at work in the morning. If Phil Dixon had no idea he was suspected, and everything indicated that this was so, a few more hours would not matter.

As he drove through the deserted Sunday streets he wondered how much longer forensics would take with the rest of the information. Nowadays so many things could be pinpointed, perhaps even the actual spot where the murder was committed. It would be helpful to know that – someone could have been in the area, their memory might be jogged. No, it was probably too late. How many innocent people would recall where they were on that Monday night?

Huntingdon, where the lab was situated, should be able to tell them the type of soil or mud which must be adhering to the underside of the car. Some would be from the compound, but the tests were sophisticated enough to show if the earth was contaminated by chemicals or weed-killer. All they then had to do was question the local farmers about what they used on their land. Not all of it, he knew, stayed within the boundary of a field.

He would also have another chat with Brian Lord and see what he made of a jack being used as a murder weapon. Ian doubted it would be very much. Like himself, he would have to believe it was a spur-of-the-moment killing. A psychological profile on such a person would encompass the whole of the human race.

11

'In a better mood, are we?' Moira asked when he came in and found her washing mud off her hands under the tap in the kitchen sink.

'What've you been up to?'

'I cleared that patch of ground at the bottom of the garden. It's been annoying me for ages. I'm going to make a compost heap.'

None of this was of any interest to Ian. He knew that their garden, in the summer, was pretty, and he enjoyed the runner beans Moira grew. To him it was a place to sit on a balmy evening, and the gradual taming of the wilderness that had been at the back when they first bought the house was all thanks to his wife.

'Do you want to go out anywhere tonight?'

'Again?'

'Yes. Again. Why not?'

'To eat or what?'

'If you like.' It was no trouble to Ian to put two meals a day away.

'Not much choice on a Sunday. A curry, I suppose.'

'I hoped you'd say that. Oh, and guess what?'

'Go on, tell me.'

'Barry's getting married.'

'No!'

'Yes. We're invited. Some time in the summer.'

'You know, Ian,' Moira said later as she spooned some mango chutney on to a piece of poppadom, 'you've been saying that this man, Daniels, had little chance of meeting married women, apart from in the pub.'

'Yes. But it's still only an assumption he had any woman, married or not.'

'All right, but had you thought of it from another angle?' She bit into the crispy starter and, as nearly always happened, it broke and some dropped on to the plate, along with the chutney.

'What angle?' Ian was interested. Often his wife was capable of doing just that, seeing another angle. As an outsider she was not confused by statements and procedures.

'How many pubs do you know that are run by single men?'

'You mean the wife of a landlord? Good God, Moira, it hadn't occurred to me.' And it hadn't. And all the time he'd been telling himself the man's only social recreation was in public houses.

'And it might explain away the food, mightn't it? If he was in the pub, she might have cooked or heated up something for him as a special favour.'

Ian took a sip of his wine. He was not a man to drink lager with a curry and couldn't understand those who did. And you could never get any decent beer in an Indian restaurant.

Rapidly he ran through the various pubs in the town. There were quite a number of them. And then another thought struck him. The Station Arms. Hadn't one of the men said he was staying there? And that was run by a lone female. Gladys, or Gloria, he thought her name was. And the man lodging there was Tom Clancey who had made a point of coming in to say he'd overheard an argument between Thomas and Daniels. Had he done so simply to divert attention away from himself? Had Clancey got a thing going with the landlady and had Daniels muscled in? It seemed highly unlikely. Men who worked away from home and indulged in extra-marital affairs (if Clancey was married, he couldn't remember) were unlikely to become seriously upset over such a matter. They knew their time in a place was limited, that there would be other women in other towns willing to oblige. It was, however, still a possibility. And today, all of a sudden, there were several possibilities.

DCI Roper was wrong on all counts, as he was to find out before the next morning.

Earlier in the week Nichola Dixon had sat in the doctor's waiting-room, her face hidden behind a five-month-old copy of *Cosmopolitan* magazine which she was not reading. She was only there to have her worst fears confirmed and to learn, which she had not successfully been able to do from Debbie, how to go about getting an abortion.

She hardly knew her GP, she was a healthy young woman, but she supposed her age would make an abortion possible, whatever his personal views. Ten minutes past her appointment time she felt like walking out, ostrich-like. If it was not confirmed, it could not be true. The dread of the internal examination she was sure she'd be subjected to was nothing compared with having to break the news to her parents. Unless, and she knew it was an impossible hope, there was some way she could have the operation without them finding out. She was not aware that a legal guardian was required to sign the necessary consent forms.

Not long after, she left the surgery holding back tears. The test was simple. A urine sample was all that was required. The GP said he was also sending it to Rickenham General to make absolutely certain. He had not passed judgement but asked what she wanted to do. She was very surprised that he made no mention of her age. It was his air of kindness and concern which caused the tears. She would have preferred to be shouted at.

She had told Paul, wanting him to believe it was his child, but when she mentioned an abortion he was horrified. The idea had been for him to lend her money so she could attend a private clinic somewhere and have it done as a day patient. Debbie had told her that much. She would miss a day's school, write a note to say she was sick. She had never had a day off before and because of her standing with the teachers it would be believed. And they had not seen her mother's handwriting.

The other alternative seemed to have failed. The real father was unlikely to believe her and, without causing herself enormous embarrassment, there was no way in which she could contact him. She was still smarting from his treatment of her. Why had he dropped her so casually? There was no question he was the child's father; only with him had she not used contraceptives.

Paul was no longer speaking to her either. He, too, was hurt, but worse, he was shocked that she had lied about her age and was aware that he could be in serious legal trouble.

But Paul was neurotic, getting so upset about so many things lately, and the fun had gone out of their relationship. He used to make her laugh; now he seemed constantly on edge and he shook. Perhaps he was drinking too much.

Whatever the reasons she knew, by Sunday morning, that she had to see him again. She would make one last-ditch attempt to talk him into lending her the money. She would not accept it as a gift, she wanted no obligations. Her own savings amounted to fifty-eight pounds, which would not go far.

To please her mother and make her less suspicious, she ate some breakfast and managed to be sick without Marie noticing. She offered to go to the shop for the paper and used the public telephone box to ring Paul. He agreed to meet her later. He was missing her and had decided that, after all he'd been through, he could not give up now. Just as soon as she was sixteen he would marry her and they would bring up their child together. University wasn't such a big deal. He would make Nicky happy.

'Push your hair back, Kate,' Marie was saying as Nicky came in via the kitchen door. 'You'll damage your eyesight.' She was aware that her daughter hid beneath her heavy fringe, still at that awkward stage when her body was developing and she was clumsy and self-conscious. Nichola had been the same. It would pass.

'Thanks, Nicky.' Marie took the paper.

'I'm just going to ring Sally. Will you mind if I go to her place? There's some notes of hers I need.'

'No, of course not.'

Consequently Nicky was out when DCI Roper and DS Swan arrived. Had she not been, the results of the events of the rest of the day could have been avoided.

Kate took herself off to her grandmother's, where she spent a lot of her time.

Nicky picked up the receiver and held it between her shoulder and neck as she tapped out a number with one hand and kept the rest depressed with the other. She spoke into silence, making arrangements with a non-existent Sally at the other end.

'I'll get the next bus, Mum.'

'What time'll you be back?'

'I'm not sure. I'll ring you.'

'Bye, love. Nicky!' she called her back. 'Take your coat, for goodness sake. It's not summer yet.'

She met Paul in the town centre and, now that it seemed there was nothing to lose, agreed to have a drink in one of the pubs. Her age was not questioned by the woman serving.

'Paul, you've got to help me. I'm desperate.'

'Nicky, I can't do it. I can't take . . .' but he stopped and bit the skin around the nail of his index finger. She noticed his hands then. Not only were they calloused from his work, the nails chipped, but there were patches of raw redness where he had chewed the skin. 'You don't seem to understand how much I love you. I'll wait. When you're old enough we'll get married. I wish you hadn't lied to me.'

She sipped her drink. She had not said when she would be home. This might take all afternoon, but she had to persuade him. The GP had suggested she talk things over with her parents. It might come to that, but not until she had made every effort with Paul.

'Shall we go back to your flat?'

His eyes lit up when she suggested it. He'd imagined he'd only have an hour with her. 'What about your parents?'

'They're out. It'll be all right.'

Nicky rarely watched television, only occasionally something between eight and nine o'clock in the evening. Neither did she read newspapers; she scoffed at the local one, imagining it was full of details of Women's Institute meetings and letters to the gardening page.

In Paul's room she sat on the bed and picked up the *Rickenham Herald* while he went to pour them a drink. Only then did she read the article about Gerry Daniels' death.

Kate came back from her grandmother's in time to share a sandwich lunch with her mother. 'Do you want to do anything this afternoon or shall we slop in front of the television?'

'Slop,' Kate said. 'And I've still got some homework to do.' The girls were different in this respect. Nicky got hers out of the way as soon as possible; Kate left it until the last minute.

'Wasn't too bad,' Marie said, switching off the set at the end of the film. 'You go and get that homework done now and I'll prepare the meal.' She looked at her watch. Nicky hadn't rung yet. Marie hoped she wouldn't be too late because she preferred them to sit at the table together to eat. Mostly sit in Nicky's case. She had not yet told her elder daughter that she had made an appointment with their GP. Come hell or high water she was going to take her there after school next week and see if he could persuade her to eat a bit more.

The meal was prepared. A chicken casserole simmered on the stove and a pan of chopped cabbage was washed and salted ready to cook.

Kate's homework was complete. They sat once more in front of the television set. 'If she doesn't ring soon I'm going to ring her,' Marie said, beginning to get annoyed. There were still two more buses to go but she did not fancy driving into Rickenham to pick up her daughter. It was unlike her to be thoughtless but lately she wasn't the same girl at all.

The next bus was a few minutes late leaving Rickenham. Marie opened the door and glanced up the road when she heard it round the corner. It didn't stop. Nichola was not on it.

'I'll murder her when she gets in,' she muttered, picking up the phone to dial Sally's parents' number which was in the diary kept next to it.

'No.' Sally's mother sounded surprised. 'I can't help you, I'm afraid. Did she say she was coming here? We haven't seen Nicky since last Sunday.' Marie replaced the receiver, worry beginning to gnaw at her stomach.

Finally, after what seemed like an eternity, the last bus ground to a noisy halt at the end of the road. Marie had been watching for it from one of the front windows. She flung open the door as relief spread warmly through her whole body. The bus remained stationary as an elderly lady struggled off it, using a walking stick as an aid. Behind her was an equally elderly man. He took her arm and they waved to the driver who pressed a button to shut the automatic doors before he pulled away.

Marie stood watching until it was out of sight, still unable to believe Nicky was not on that one either.

Kate looked up and saw her mother's pale, worried face and sensed that something terrible must have happened.

'She wasn't on it?'

'No. Kate, did she say anything to you, anything at all, about where she was going?'

'No. Honestly, Mum, I'd've told you.' She paused. 'She was crying in her room the other day though.'

'Crying?'

'Yes. But she wouldn't tell me what the matter was. She said I wasn't to tell you.'

Only then did it dawn on Marie what the matter might be. How stupid she was not to see it before. Nicky's paleness, her not eating, the change in her character. She had to be on drugs.

After the curry, which had been better than of late, they returned home. Mark graced them with his company and they watched TV together until quite late. For once there were several programmes which the Ropers agreed upon watching.

'I'm going to have a brandy to help digest that food,' Moira informed her husband.

'Finest excuse I've ever heard. Pour me one too, love, would you?'

'Do you want something, Mark? A glass of wine?'

'No thanks.' Both his parents had, from quite a young age, allowed him a sip of whatever they were drinking. They believed it avoided problems later. Mark hated the taste of all spirits and they were pleased it stayed that way. Sometimes he'd have a glass of wine or a glass of his father's Adnams which Moira bought in large plastic

bottles from the supermarket. Ian would have been morti-
fied, not to know that his son occasionally drank alcohol in
pubs – his face was still too babyish to get away with it
often – but that he drank lager.

They went to bed quite late and Ian knew he would
regret it in the morning. The sound of the alarm clock was
one he dreaded.

He had been asleep an hour and a half when the telephone rang. He thought his heart had stopped until he
realised it was beating loudly and rapidly in his chest.
'Sodding thing,' he said as he reached for the bedside
light.

It had to be work. Mark was safely in bed, Moira was
beside him and the only other person they had to be concerned about was Moira's mother who, at just turned
sixty, was brimming with health, very active and, like her
daughter, looked years younger than her age.

'Okay. I'm on my way.'

'What is it?' Moira asked sleepily.

'I'm not sure, but it's to do with the Daniels case. I've
got to go in, I'm afraid. I'll try not to disturb you if
I'm back before morning.' He knew he would not
have been disturbed himself at this hour unless it was
important.

Ian was aware how noisy a car engine sounded in the
dead hours of a winter's night. It couldn't be helped.
Hopefully his neighbours were too deeply asleep to hear
it. If they did, and bothered to get out of bed to see what
was going on, they would realise there was some sort of
emergency on and forgive him. Hopefully.

The journey took no time at all. He passed only one other
vehicle, and that was a police car. The engine had still not
had a chance to warm up by the time he reached the
station and he was bitterly cold.

Shivering and tired, he already wished he'd gone to bed
earlier and had had at least four hours' sleep. He went

174

through the revolving door, the lights from inside like a beacon in the surrounding darkness.

Apart from one officer behind the desk, the place felt deserted.

'Fill me in,' he said to the PC who had magically appeared and who had probably been watching out for his car.

'It started with a call from a worried mother of a teenage daughter,' PC Geoffries said as they walked briskly together down the hallway. 'She was expecting her back at the latest at seven but she wasn't on the last bus. They live out at Frampton. The name's Dixon.'

Ian stopped in his tracks. 'What?'

'Dixon. Nichola Dixon, that's the girl's name. The mother rang everyone she could think of, including the parents of another girl who Nichola was supposed to be visiting.'

'In here,' Ian said, opening the door of an empty office and switching on the light.

'Once she'd done that, she contacted us. We sent someone straight over and got a description of what she was wearing and a photograph. She's fifteen.'

'Oh my God.'

'It's all right, sir. She's safe. She's here.'

There had to be more to it than that. They would not have thought it necessary to call him in to say a missing girl had been found. They would not have even telephoned.

'Patrol car spotted her. She was wandering around aimlessly and obviously very drunk.' This was no huge surprise. There had been numerous cases of under-age drinking and it seemed to be on the increase.

'What happened?'

'At first she refused to get in the car, and you know what it's like with minors, try to help them, and they, or the parents, get nasty. The men were aware she was missing and said they were taking her home. She became

175

hysterical, screaming and shouting and telling them to leave her alone. Then she started on about some fellow who's made her pregnant.'

'At fifteen.' It was not a question. The implications of the consequences of her age were in his tone. 'And?'

'And this fellow, she claims, was Gerry Daniels.'

'Oh, my God,' Ian repeated. Phillip Dixon looked more of a suspect than ever.

Nichola Dixon did not look so pretty now. Her face was puffy and blotchy with both tears and alcohol. Sitting in an interview room with only a silent WPC for company, she no longer felt like a woman but more like the child she really was. She would have given anything to wipe out the past six months and to start again. To have her mother put her to bed and tell her everything was going to be all right was all she wanted. Except it was not all right. She was fifteen and pregnant and drunk; the father of her child was dead and now her mother was certain to discover her condition. The father of the child was not only dead, he had been murdered. And she was being held in a police station. They might even think she'd killed him.

And Paul had known about Gerry. Still she couldn't understand how. He had almost gloated when he looked over her shoulder as she was reading the article. No wonder she had not seen Gerry those nights she waited outside the compound fence, watching the men come up. He had already been dead a week then.

No one had come over to her and told her. Some of the men had seen her before. After that first time, when, out of curiosity, she had stopped to see what they were doing, and Gerry had called out to her, then come across to speak to her, she often paused on her way to the bus stop. His afternoon break mostly coincided with the time she came out of school. Once or twice someone had whistled at her.

The third cup of coffee was beginning to sober her up. She was aware that her mother was somewhere in the building, possibly Kate too. Gran couldn't be expected to take her in in the middle of the night. Why couldn't she see her yet? And why had no one asked her any questions? Perhaps they weren't allowed to unless someone was with her, like on the television, a solicitor or something.

But there was light at the end of the tunnel. The truth would come out in front of witnesses, it would give her mother a chance to take it in before they went home. If they let her go home.

'Mrs Dixon's in there.' PC Geoffries thumbed towards a door which was partially closed. 'She's been given coffee and someone's watching the other daughter. She had no one to leave her with.'

'Okay, Geoffries, thanks. I'll see her now.'

The Chief pushed open the door and was shocked to see the change in Marie Dixon. She looked grey and exhausted and her hair fell lankly around her face.

'Mrs Dixon, you remember me?'

Marie nodded numbly.

'The main thing is your daughter's safe.'

'I know, but what was she thinking of? It's drugs, isn't it? I've been so stupid. She hasn't been eating and she looks so pale. I read all those leaflets but I still didn't see it.'

'Drugs? What makes you say that?'

'It has to be, doesn't it?' She was resigned to the fact.

'Not necessarily. I haven't spoken to your daughter yet – we can't talk to her without your being there, Mrs Dixon – but it might be wise to inform you that we believe her to be under the influence of alcohol, and she is quite distressed. I'd better warn you in advance that we will have to question her about Gerry Daniels, the man who was murdered recently.'

177

'Whatever for?'

'She may have known him.'

'That's impossible.'

'If you'd like to come with me, we'll see your daughter now.'

The reasons for Nichola being detained were explained to her a second time, in the presence of her legal guardian. She said she understood.

Many thoughts raced through the Chief's head as he walked with Marie Dixon the short distance to the interview room. A whole new light had been thrown on the case now. If what Nichola claimed was true, he had been near in believing that the Dixon family was involved. It explained Daniels' knowledge of Marie's surname; Nichola must surely have spoken about her family. No doubt Thomas, in his mild paranoia, only heard the name Dixon and jumped to his own conclusions.

'Hello, Nichola. My name's Ian Roper. Can I call you Nichola, or Nicky?'

She appeared not to hear him as she looked at her mother, her eyes filling with tears. 'Mum.' It came out as a sob. Marie glanced at the Chief, who nodded an affirmative. Marie went over to her daughter and put her arms around her.

'Nicky, Nicky, what have you been doing?' She stroked her hair back. 'I've been worried sick.'

'Mrs Dixon, would you like to take a seat? It's late, the sooner we get this over with, the sooner you can go home.' This was not going to be easy. It did not appear that Marie Dixon was aware of Nichola's condition. He took a deep breath and explained the form the interview would take, who was present and the time and the date.

'Can you tell us where you were tonight, Nicky?'

'I went to a friend's house. Not Sally's. I told Mum I was going to Sally's. I didn't.'

'Which friend?'

'His name's Paul Adamson.'

'Is Paul your boyfriend?'

Nicky's eyes went back to where Marie sat before she answered. 'Yes. Sort of.'

'Have you known him long?'

'About six months.'

'Oh, why didn't –'

'Please, Mrs Dixon. It's important we ask these questions.'

'I'm sorry.'

'I'm sorry, too, that I have to ask these things, but we do need to know. What was your relationship with Paul Adamson?' It might be he who had got her pregnant; the relationship with Daniels, an older, experienced, handsome man, might be wishful thinking.

'Do you mean sex? Yes, I slept with him.' There was a gasp from Marie but she did not speak.

'And tonight, what did you do?'

'I met him at lunchtime and went to his flat. We had some drinks and then . . . and then I read that Gerry had been killed. I thought he didn't want to see me. I didn't know.'

'One thing at a time, Nicky. You read that Gerry was dead. What did you do next?'

'I was upset. Paul was sneering. I went round to see Debbie and when the pubs opened we went out. She knew one where they don't make you go at ten thirty. I didn't want to go home, I wanted to die.'

'And then the police car stopped and they brought you here?'

'Yes.'

'That's fine. Now tell me about Gerry Daniels.'

She did so, explaining how he had come to talk to her at the fence, that she thought he was so very handsome. 'I knew he was too old for me but I told him I was seventeen.' Ian did not question this. Even now, childlike in her pathos, she still looked older than her years.

'And you eventually went out with him?'

'Yes. Several times. He knew I couldn't be late. We'd go out in the country for a drink and sometimes something to eat. He was always hungry. I couldn't understand why he wasn't there. I waited by the compound several times after school.'

'Think carefully, Nichola – when did you last see him?'

'Monday night. Last Monday night. We went to the Stag and Hounds because they're open all day for food.'

Ian had been holding his breath. Now he knew where Daniels had eaten his last meal. It was one of those road houses where the food, he suspected, came ready prepared and only needed microwaving. All very basic stuff served from midday until ten at night. Daniels had obviously taken her there straight from work. The men, he recalled, had left work an hour early that Monday because a lorry had not turned up with more rings to line the tunnel.

'Can you remember what you ate?'

'I had scampi, I wasn't really hungry. Gerry had roast beef, he asked for extra vegetables. It didn't look very nice though.'

'And how did he pay?'

'Cash. I know that, because afterwards he called in at the Red Lion – he wanted to borrow some money, I think. I waited in the car.' This, then, explained his brief appearance there. If he paid cash it would be harder to check Nicky's story.

'What time was it then?'

'Oh, about seven, or just after.'

'What did you do after that?'

Nichola stared at her hands which were clasped tightly in her lap. 'We went for a drive.'

'I know this is difficult for you, but did he touch you? Try to kiss you or anything?'

'More than that.'

'More?'

'I, we, did it. In the car. I had to be home soon after that. He dropped me at the bus stop, the one just before I get off. He didn't just leave me there, he parked up the road and watched until I was on it.'

He parked up the road. Out near Frampton. Just before you get to the village. And that was where the jack was found.

'This might seem an odd question, Nicky, but was his car all right? I mean, did he get a flat tyre or anything?'

She looked puzzled. 'No. Oh, he said something about checking the oil in the morning and he was going to get the can out of the boot to remind himself.'

'So the last time you saw him was when you got on the bus, and he was sitting in the car?'

'He got out just then, to get the oil, I suppose. He waved to me but I didn't wave back in case there was anyone on the bus who knew me. I didn't wave back.' She started to cry again. Ian decided to let her. 'He took me out and bought me a meal and then he gets killed and I didn't even wave back.'

'It's all right, Nicky. Can you tell me which bus you were on?'

'The one that leaves Rickenham at quarter to nine.'

Marie sat silently throughout the exchange of questions and answers. She was hardly able to believe what she was hearing. How little she knew her daughter.

When Nicky seemed calmer, Ian asked the question he had been putting off. 'You said something to the officers who brought you here, something about Gerry Daniels. Can you remember what it was?' Coward, he told himself.

'I'm pregnant.' The look of terror on her face as she said this was enough to soften the heart of the hardest interrogator. She waited, unblinking, until her mother spoke.

'You should have told me, Nicky. I'm not a monster. We can sort it out.' At least it wasn't drugs, was the one hopeful thought in her head. 'You should've come to me.'

'I asked Paul for the money for an abortion,' she said, the exchange now between mother and daughter. 'He wouldn't give it to me. Come to you? How could I? You were too busy with that boyfriend of yours. So don't get all sentimental and everything and pretend what a wonderful mother you are. Everyone on the site knows about it. You and that man Neil.'

'Nichola!'

'Don't deny it, it's true.' Ian had begun feeling sorry for the girl with her various problems, but now he was seeing another side of her. 'And if you tell Dad about any of this, I'll tell him about you.'

There was total silence as they all gazed at the pretty girl. It crossed one or two minds that if she was capable of blackmail, she might also be capable of murder. However, she was far too slight to have moved the body and, presumably, she couldn't drive.

'If only he was here now,' Marie said. Never had she needed Phil so much.

'With a bit of luck he could be soon.'

'Pardon?' She stared at Ian in bewilderment. 'He's not due back for ages. You've . . .' She looked from him to her daughter. It didn't matter now what Nicky said. Phil was to be interviewed and it would all come out. 'I'm sorry, Nicky. What we've both done is wrong. It's over between me and Neil. I shall tell Dad myself, there'll be no more lies. He cares for you, you know that, he won't throw you on the street, and neither shall I.'

'Mrs Dixon, you and your daughter have a lot of things to sort out. It might be best to sleep on it. I've just got one more question then I'll get someone to drive you home. Nicky, can you be sure the child you're carrying is Mr Daniels'?' It mattered. It might be that Dixon thought his wife was having an affair with him, or his daughter, or both, and if the daughter was pregnant, even more reason to kill him.

'Yes. We didn't take any precautions. I didn't think it would matter.' Ian had heard that a few times. 'I am positive.'

'Okay, that's it for now.'

He made a note of Paul Adamson's address and organised a car. 'What did you make of that?' he asked he WPC, who had remained throughout the interview.

'Makes me glad I've only got sons.'

Paul Adamson lay awake knowing he had blown it. He had had Nicky to himself for the whole afternoon and early evening and ten minutes after they got to the flat he had started making those spiteful comments. She had run out, half crying, and he didn't think he would see her again. She must have liked Daniels more than he thought to react like that.

Paul could not know that it was not his death that upset her so much as the fact that he was dead. Nicky had planned to ask Gerry for the abortion money, threatening him with her age if necessary.

When the police knocked at his door at 6.30 a.m. on Monday it seemed almost inevitable, somehow.

Ian crawled back into bed at six. He had left his instructions knowing he was too tired to be of any use.

A gentle breeze had ruffled his hair as he quietly shut the car door. It was like an omen. The worst of the winter and the case were over.

Moira hardly stirred but was subconsciously aware of his presence because she reversed into him, as he called it, resting her bottom in the curve of his stomach and bent legs. When he woke up she was gone and the house was silent. It was ten fifteen.

Luxuriating in having the bathroom to himself, he took a hot shower and shaved, then made some toast and a pot of tea. An hour later he was back at headquarters.

'Nothing for you to do,' DS Swan informed him. 'All signed and sealed.'

'Adamson?'

'Yes. You had a hectic Sunday, I hear?'

'Yes. Quite. But as you're looking so spruce and rested, you can do the donkey work today.'

'Not that rested. We didn't get home until late.'

'Oh, yes, the pre-nuptial celebrations.'

Ian had drunk two mugs of strong tea; his body told him it now required coffee. They went to the canteen.

'Headache not gone, dear?' Betty, behind the counter, inquired solicitously.

'Yes. Why?'

'Oh, just that you don't look so hot today.' Ian hated that. If people told him he did not look well he began to believe them.

'Do I need to see him, Adamson?'

'No. We've got a confession. Seems like now he knows he can't have Nichola, nothing else matters to him.'

'What's he like?'

'Difficult to say. Obsessed, I think. It's like nothing but Nichola is important. He seems more upset by her lying about her age than about what he's done.'

'I wonder what that argument was about, between Thomas and Daniels?'

'Don't suppose we'll ever know. My guess is Thomas got the wrong end of the stick. Daniels probably learned of the affair from Nicky and he used it to wind him up. Thomas, being the sort of man he is, would probably assume the only way Daniels would know Marie's surname was if he was seeing her himself.'

'Is Adamson's statement typed up?'

'Should be by now.'

'Bring it up when it's ready, will you?'

Paul Adamson's statement was straightforward. All the way through it were constant references to Nichola Dixon and how much he loved her.

'I saw her one afternoon,' he said. 'The weather was foul and I had to pack up work. I knew what time she came out of school and which bus stop she used. I drove down there. She'd never let me give her a lift home but I thought she might let me take her part of the way. At least I'd see her. She was there, all right, standing up by the wire fence, talking to some man. She was laughing and flicking her hair back like she does, teasing, you know. I felt sick, I was so jealous. I went there another time and saw her again. Then she told me she was going round to Debbie's one Monday night. It was a stupid lie. Me and Wayne used to go round there all the time with the girls. I waited outside the school and I followed her. I was right behind them in the car. I know it was dark, but she was so wrapped up in him she never even noticed me. I waited outside the restaurant and followed them again.' There had been a long pause here. Paul needed to get himself together. He was reliving those moments after Daniels' car had pulled off the road and he realised just what they were doing inside it. 'She got on the bus. I was going to follow him again but he got out of the car. He was getting something out of the boot. He was surprised to see anyone. He said, "Hello." He was smiling. The bastard was actually smiling, like he knew who I was. I asked if I could borrow his tools, I said I'd got a flat tyre. He handed me the jack and offered to help. I hit him with it. I don't know if I meant to kill him or not. I don't even know if he was dead when I put him in the boot. And I didn't care.'

'What did you do next?' the interviewing officer asked.

'I drove his car back to where he worked. I was going to leave it there but by then I was really scared. I thought if I could get him down that hole there it would look like an accident.'

'But the compound is lit at night and there's a security guard.'

'I didn't know about the guard, I didn't see anyone, and the gate was open. I didn't think about anyone seeing me. I drove right up to that circular thing.'

'The shaft?'

'Yeah, I suppose so. I only had to lift him a couple of extra feet.'

Paul had put his arms under Gerry's armpits and hauled his body to a position on the safety wall. It had been easy enough to tip him over. 'I left his car there.'

'And *your* car?'

'I went back for it on the last bus. Nicky was mine,' he almost shouted. 'Can't you understand that? I'd've made her so happy. That man was no good for her.'

'So,' Ian said, 'I'm beginning to see how his mind worked. He whacks Daniels and at that stage is still in a state of shock. That's why he chucks the jack away. Only as he begins to drive does the solution come to him: he's going to try to make it look like an accident. The first bit I can go along with, the rest, well, it's a bit coldblooded for someone who claims not to know or care what he's doing.'

'Panic sometimes makes for total lucidity,' Barry said.

'Maybe. Anyway, we know now Daniels didn't bother to change because he would be wasting time. Nicky had to be in early. That puzzled me a lot, him wearing his working gear.'

'And the rest of it, it's plausible. With those pumps going Phillips, the guard or whatever, probably didn't hear a car, or if he did, thought it belonged to that bloke in the caravan. Kavanagh?'

'Yes. Kavanagh. Another piece of luck, him being out.'

'Not really. When he was interviewed the second time he admitted there had been many other occasions, and if he had been there he'd have had a skinful to drink, and his curtains were permanently drawn.'

Paul Adamson ended his statement by saying he didn't care about anything except Nicky and he was glad the bastard was dead. Ian hoped, for Adamson's sake, that he did not express this view before he was sentenced.

Phil Dixon let himself into his house as soon as he had been to the police. He had been easily traced and had returned to England immediately, leaving his lorry at a foreign depot and taking a flight. He had nothing to fear; he could fly back the next day and complete the job. From Ian's point of view, it was too late to stop him. Having found him, they always seemed to be one step behind and he was already on the plane before they realised exactly where he was. He arrived late on the Monday evening and was told his presence was no longer required.

Marie, white-faced, explained the whole situation. Phil, who had turned away advances throughout the course of his marriage, had never experienced anguish such as this. The pain was unimaginable, but real. He listened until his wife finished what she had to say then picked up his holdall, which contained a change of underwear and a gift for each of his family, and walked out of the door.

He did not tell her what he had done: there was no point now. Cyril George had agreed to his three months' notice. Phil was a good driver but there were plenty more and Cyril understood he wanted a job nearer home, nearer his wife, so as they could see more of each other.

Tired as he was, he found a place to stay the night, then made the long journey back to the airport at the crack of dawn. As soon as this trip was over he would speak to Cyril, see if he couldn't continue as he was.

For the moment, his life was over.

Marie did not wait until Phil came home. First thing on Monday morning, having spent what remained of the night sitting in an armchair downstairs, she rang Neil at work, not caring if anyone else answered the phone. He seemed unable to comprehend what she was saying. When it sank in, he begged her to change her mind. He could not believe it was over.

Strangely, when he returned to Marg that night, he did not experience the misery and loneliness he had imagined he would feel. He waited for the sense of loss to hit him. It didn't. What he did feel was a sense of relief. He had lived his whole life by the book and, apart from this one thing, had done nothing shocking, immoral, illegal or even vaguely out of the ordinary. He was not cut out for it. When Marg laid her swollen hand on his thigh he didn't even flinch.

Within twenty-four hours it was as if the affair had never been.

With each passing week the weather became milder. Snowdrops gave way to daffodils, then tulips. Primroses lined the banks and hedgerows and hawthorn flowered in red and white.

Moira's garden flourished. The runner beans began the intricate winding of their tendrils around the bamboo canes and, as the heat of the sun increased, impatiens and lobelia spilled out over the sides of their tubs.

'Only six more weeks,' Mark said, 'and you'll be shot of me.' His exams were over and he was confident he had done well. There was a provisional place waiting for him at an art college in September, dependent upon his grades.

'Do you realise,' Moira overheard a woman in the check-out queue in Safeway's saying, 'we're nearer next Christmas now than last?'

The football season started again. Earlier each year, it seemed to Moira. There was one thing to be grateful for, the World Cup was over. Give Ian his due, he had hardly watched any of it. Crime had its plus points.

Mark failed his driving test but passed on his second attempt when he was lucky enough to get a cancellation. Moira chose her moment carefully. Ian, delighted that Norwich had knocked up another win, agreed to purchase a second car. They decided to go for something reasonably priced, but safe. Mark would be taking it to college with him. On the following weekend they found a B-registered Ford Fiesta that fitted the bill. They were not unduly concerned about the odd bit of rust.

They paid cash and took the car away with them, Moira driving it, Ian in his own. To get home they had to go through the town centre via Saxborough Road.

The scars on the landscape had virtually healed. Four sets of temporary traffic lights had disappeared and the roadworks that went with the operation were complete. There were patches of new tarmac everywhere.

The Water Board were relieved at the number of complaints, which after the initial onslaught had dwindled as people began to accept the inevitable. Only a few genuine claims had been made. They were not holding their breath, though. They knew what to expect when the inflated water rates demands were sent out.

Moira tooted to Ian as he took a left to go home and she continued on to do some shopping. She rather liked the car and was sorry she couldn't have it permanently. At least she'd be able to use it in the holidays.

She drove straight on and into the car-park where the shaft had once been. It had, as was part of the agreement, been flattened, resurfaced and neatly marked in rectangles in white paint. Heat from the tarmac bounced up in waves as she got out and locked the door.

Tomorrow, she thought as she fumbled for her shopping list, I must buy something for Barry's wedding. Her mind was on colours and styles as she headed towards the automatic doors and the welcome air-conditioning.

There was no way she could have known that two hundred feet or so beneath the B-registered Ford Fiesta was the spot where Gerry Daniels' body had been found.

DE